The Faerie Hills

A MUIRTEACH MacPHEE MYSTERY

THE FAERIE HILLS

SUSAN MCDUFFIE

FIVE STAR
A part of Gale, Cengage Learning

GALE
CENGAGE Learning

Detroit • New York • San Francisco • New Haven, Conn • Waterville, Maine • London

GALE
CENGAGE Learning™

LIBRARY OF CONGRESS CATALOGING-IN-PUBLICATION DATA

McDuffie, Susan.
  The Faerie Hills: a Muirteach MacPhee mystery / Susan McDuffie. — 1st ed.
    p. cm.
  ISBN-13: 978-1-59414-961-0 (hardcover)
  ISBN-10: 1-59414-961-5 (hardcover)
  1. Children—Crimes against—Fiction. 2. Colonsay (Scotland)—Fiction. 3. Scotland—History—1057–1603—Fiction. I. Title.
  PS3613.C396F34 2011
  813'.6—dc22   2010051990

First Edition. First Printing: April 2011.
Published in 2011 in conjunction with Tekno Books and Ed Gorman.

Printed in the United States of America
1 2 3 4 5 6 7 15 14 13 12 11

ACKNOWLEDGMENTS

Thanks go to so many people, especially Rafe Martin, Robin Dunlap, Donna Lake, and June Stevens for reading the initial manuscript and making helpful suggestions, and to Paterson Simons of Simons Fine Art (www.simonsfineart.com) for his wonderful work on the maps. Thanks also go to George and Fiona Eogan and the Archaeological Institute for the amazing and inspiring tour of Ireland and stories of Bronze Age gold. Lastly, thanks to my parents, Bruce and Wini McDuffie, for their loving encouragement of a daughter who believed in fairies.

The Faerie Hills was partially inspired by the Bridget Cleary case in 1890s Ireland. A man, convinced his wife had been "taken" by the fairies, burned her to death in an attempt to drive the changeling out. This story intrigued me and I wondered what it might be like to live in a culture and a society believing so firmly in the "good people." This book is my attempt to answer that question.

COLONSAY

Nunnery

Beinn Beag △
Càrnan △ Eòin

Traigh Bàn

Gillean's House

Àine's Cottage

Riasg Buidhe

Dun Evin

Kilchattan

N
E
S
W

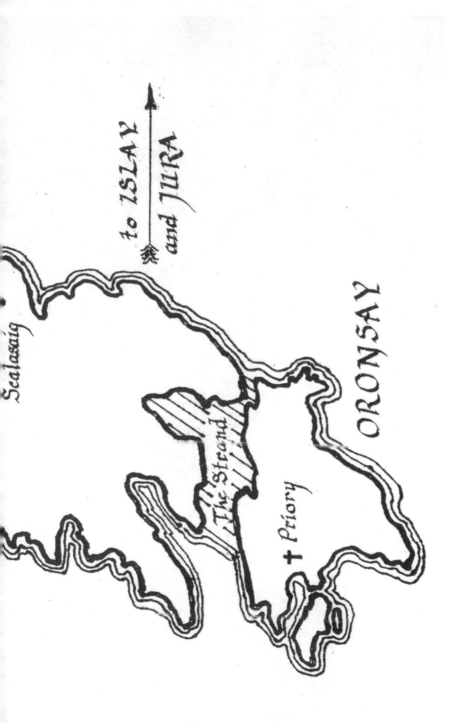

COLONSAY

Scalasaig

Gormal's
Cave

JURA

Village

Loch Tarbert

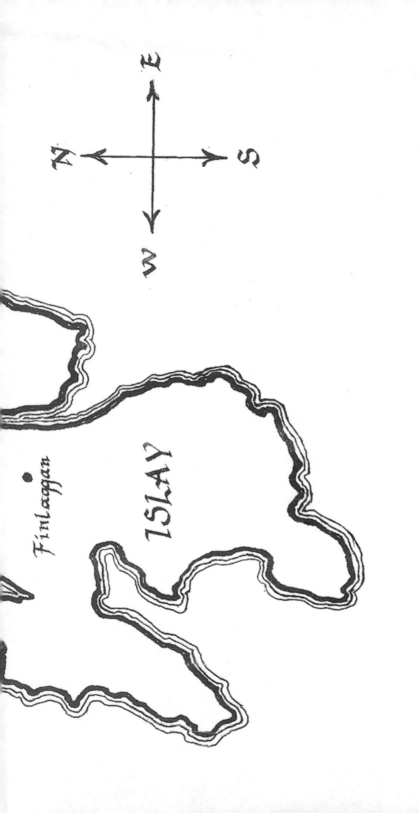

CAST OF CHARACTERS

On Colonsay

At Dun Evin
Muirteach MacPhee
Somerled, his dog
Mariota Beaton, daughter of a physician from Islay
Gillespic, Muirteach's uncle, Chief of the Clan MacPhee
Euluasaid, his wife
Dòmhnall, their son
Malcolm, Gillespic's oldest son
Niall, their foster son, grandson of the Lord of the Isles
Fergus, Gillespic's man
Rhoderick, another of Gillespic's men
Elidh, a pretty maidservant
Ranald MacDonald, Niall's father from Benbecula, and a son
  of the Lord of the Isles
Sine, Ranald's wife
Liam MacLean, visiting Colonsay from Mull
Griogair MacRuari, visiting from Uist
Raghnall MacRuari, his brother, also visiting

In Scalasaig
Seamus, Muirteach's fourteen-year-old friend
Aorig, Seamus's mother

Maire, Sean, and baby Columbanus, Muirteach's half sister
and half brothers, now living with Aorig and her family
Donald Dubh, tavern keeper

Here and there on Colonsay

Àine, Fergus's auntie
Iaian, Fergus's cousin
Gillean, a "faerie doctor"
Eachann Beag, an elderly man with a goat named Muireal
Father Gillecolm, the priest at the village of Kilchattan
Seonag, a girl from the village Riasg Buidhe
Seonag's sister
Aidan, her baby

At the nunnery at Balnahard

Sister Morag
Sister Euphemia
Abbess Brìde

On Jura

Gormal, a witch
Lulach, her son
An old village woman on Loch Tarbert
Ian and Marsali, friendly villagers

On Uist

Donal MacRuari, the Gorrie, Chief of the MacRuaris
Marsali, his daughter
Raghnall's sister

On Islay

John MacDonald, the Lord of the Isles
Fearchar Beaton, a physician
Alsoon, Muirteach's housekeeper on Islay
Her husband

GLOSSARY

Amadan (fem. Amadain): fool
Bairn: a child
Bean-Shìdh: faerie woman or faerie wife
Birlinn: Scottish galley, varying in size from a few to many oars
Brat: mantle
Cailleach: old hag
Copag: dock, a medicinal plant
Dia: God
Dia dhuit: God be with you (literally God today)
Eilean: island
Gille Mor: sword bearer
Glaiserig: the gray slinking one, a female faerie
Gruagach: the glaiserig's male companion
Leamhnach: a small yellow flower, known as tomentil or bloodroot
Leine: saffron shirt, made of linen
Luchd-tighe: chief's bodyguard
Machair: level or low land, a plain
Mazer: drinking cup
Mether: wooden square-sided drinking cup
Mo chridhe: (mo cree) my heart
Nabhaig: a small boat
Nathrach: serpent
Quaich: round saucer-like drinking cup

Samhain: the old Celtic festival falling before All Saints' Day
Sgian dubh: dagger
Sithichean: the faerie, the good folk
Sithean: a faerie hill
Uisgebeatha: whiskey (literally, the water of life)

PROLOGUE

Isle of Colonsay, October 1373

"You'll be getting a curse for sure."

The wind, blowing strongly over the golden sands of the Tràigh Bàn this morning, sent clouds overhead scudding across the sky, like lambs frolicking on a pasture of blue. The noise of the wind and the waves might have obscured the speaker's words and lost them in the breeze, for the young boy either did not hear, or chose to ignore the warning. He continued walking across the sand to the black cliffs on the north side of the bay.

"Niall, did you not hear me? You should not be digging up there." The older boy ran and easily caught up with the younger one, then grabbed him by the arm. "Father will be angry. We were to be looking for that cow."

"You are an old woman, Dòmhnall!" Niall cried as he wriggled his way out of Dòmhnall's grasp. "Aren't you wanting to know what is in the cairn there?"

The younger boy gestured up past the cliffs towards the two hills that overlooked the bay. He then looked obstinately at the older boy a moment, squinting, for the sun was bright that day and the wind brisk where it blew along the beach.

"After we are finding the treasure we can buy your father many cows. And that red one will be going back to the dun on her own—she is a smart one." Turning his back on Dòmhnall, he took a path that climbed upwards towards one of the hills.

After a bit of climbing, he stopped and turned around to catch his breath and glare at the older boy who followed behind him. "You will be coming back and taking the treasure for yourself, that is what you will be doing, Dòmhnall."

"No, no, I would never be doing that, not for the life of me. You are a fool, Niall, even to be thinking of digging into that cairn! You've heard the stories. Wasn't it young Teàrlach himself who was stolen away by the *sithichean* for merely lying down to rest upon a faerie hill?"

"I am no fool! It's you who are the fool!"

The dark-haired boy shook his head. "Not I. Whatever is there belongs to the good people, the *sithichean*. I am telling you, Niall, you should not be disturbing those things. You should listen to me, for I am older than you."

The younger boy looked at him, then smiled and said slowly, "You're afraid."

"Aye," retorted Dòmhnall, "and so should you be! The faerie are not to be trifled with."

"My grandfather is the Lord of the Isles. I am not afraid of anything!"

With that he turned away and kept climbing, followed reluctantly by his companion. Finally the boy reached his objective, a jumbled pile of rocks and turf, settled himself by the edge, pulled a small spade from his bag, and began digging away at the mound. After a time he held up something, his freckled face flushed with triumph.

"A faerie arrow! Look, Dòmhnall."

The older boy turned to look, and examined the flint arrowhead that lay in his foster brother's palm without touching it, then crossed himself.

"You should not be touching that."

Niall shook his blond head stubbornly.

"Dòmhnall, it's worse than an old woman you are. Don't you

remember himself telling us all last night about the faerie gold to be found in these mounds, how it is just waiting, just lying on the ground it is."

"That is just a story."

"No, it's wrong you are. There is faerie gold, for I was finding a piece of it myself. And I will be finding more of it. It must be here."

"There is no faerie gold, and if there were, it would be bringing bad luck with it."

The younger boy ignored him.

"Well, if you are such an *amadan*, I myself will not be. I will be going back now."

The younger boy continued his excavation while his foster-brother turned and waited a moment.

"Are you not coming with me?"

The younger boy did not answer, but kept digging.

"I'm away then," Dòmhnall declared, but with a hint of hesitation in his voice. He waited, staring at Niall, whose blond head bent intently over his excavation. Finally, hearing no reply, Dòmhnall walked away, leaving the younger boy still delving into the jumbled pile of rocks.

CHAPTER 1

The wind blew strong that day, I remember, whirling the yellow leaves, which were just beginning to fall, and setting them to dancing for some few brief moments before they touched the ground. Although I was supposed to be mending a fishing net that afternoon as I sat outside my fine new house on the Rinns, it was little enough that I was getting done on it. I let the net fall in my lap and stared at the white clouds that rushed by overhead, as if in their rapidly changing shapes I would find the answer to the disease that plagued me that day.

Truth to tell, there should have been nothing to discountenance me. I was settling in on my new lands, given me at the beginning of the summer. I had solved the murder of my father for the Lord of the Isles, thereby serving His Lordship, and helping him out of a nasty spot of potential trouble with the Holy Father in Rome, besides.

The holding on Islay was neat and well-run, a far cry from my other house in Scalasaig, and as an old couple who lived there as caretakers still stayed on, I had not yet had a chance to run it into the ground. I found myself enjoying the novelty of an ordered house and a well-filled larder. The holding lay in close proximity to the lands of Fearchar Beaton, the physician, and his daughter Mariota, and that served only to increase its attractiveness in my view.

I had seen little of Mariota that summer or during the early autumn. She had often been at Finlaggan, or Dunstaffnage, with her father, while I had been careful to keep myself out of the sphere of His Lordship's court. The MacDonald had said he would call upon me for other matters as he saw fit, and I thought it best not to be altogether too easy to find. I did not doubt he would find me quickly enough when he needed me.

Somerled dozed at my feet, his legs twitching in his sleep, as though he chased rabbits. About the only game that lazy hound did chase, I thought to myself. I idly watched two gulls fighting over a bit of fish thrown on the midden, but it was soon enough that the warm sun shining down worked on me too, and my own eyelids closed.

I could not have slept long, but I dreamed.

A dark gray mist settling over a strange rocky landscape, and through the fog a voice crying, but I could not catch the words. A child's voice it seemed to me that it was, but, before I could be sure of it, the voice was swallowed by the mist, and the fog pierced by flame, and I saw a funeral procession, walking on a rocky strand, lit by torches with the sounds of the dirge and the women keening loud in my ears.

I woke with a start. Little enough time had passed: a moment or two, no more, for the same gulls still fought in the midden and Somerled still slept at my feet. The sun looked not much further advanced than it had been, and the same clouds, their shapes but little changed, danced in the sky. I shuddered and at that moment a cloud moved over the sun and the world grew dark for an instant.

A dream was all it had been, I told myself, not a true seeing. It was my mother who had had the Sight, not myself.

But I laid the net down, and went inside where Alsoon, who kept house for me with her husband, had left some ale and bannocks on the table. I waved the flies away that buzzed around the pitcher. I took the cloth off the jug, and poured myself a beaker of ale, which I drank straightaway. I poured some more ale, and then wolfed down a bannock, but the oats tasted dry on my tongue.

Some two days after that the messengers came. Late afternoon it was, with the sun just setting in a blaze of rose and vermilion, when I saw Rhoderick walking up the path that led to my steading. A Colonsay man, one of my uncle's men. And Rhoderick had not journeyed alone. The crew of the *birlinn* Rhoderick had brought over to Islay, some twelve men, followed him.

"Alsoon," I called. "We have visitors."

Alsoon and her husband came eagerly enough, for visitors were not all that common, and so we all three were waiting, along with Somerled, when Rhoderick and the others reached the cottage.

"*Dia dhuit*," I greeted him politely enough, although my heart was sinking.

"And to you," returned Rhoderick. "You are looking well, Muirteach." He paused, and looked around the cottage. "This is a fine place, and no mistake."

I agreed, and introduced Alsoon and her husband.

"And what is the news, Rhoderick?" I asked, after he and his crew had seated themselves on the benches outside my house and finished the ale Alsoon had brought them. I did not think these men carried good news with them. "What is bringing you Colonsay men so far from Dun Evin this evening?"

Rhoderick looked at the ground, his red hair not hiding a bit of bald spot on the top of his head. "It is bad news that we are bringing, Muirteach, and no mistake."

The oarsmen suddenly fell silent. The sunset seemed to cast a reddish glow over the whitewashed wall of my cottage while I waited for him to continue.

"It is young Niall. The boy your uncle is fostering for that Ranald MacDonald from Benbecula, the one who holds Borve

Castle on that tiny island. His Lordship's own son, off that Amie MacRuari. Niall will be Ranald's third son, fostered at your uncle's. So he is grandson to His Lordship himself. The boy's gone missing."

I thought of young Niall, the grandson of the Lord of the Isles. A late son of his father, he had only eight years and a wild adventurous streak in him. Bad enough to have a young lad go missing, but for the boy to be the grandson of the MacDonald made an additional, unwelcome tangle in the skein. The Lord of the Isles was our overlord, chief of the Clan MacDonald, and ruler of a confederation of clans that stretched across the Hebrides and into the mainland. A powerful man, and a canny one, as I had learned that previous summer after my father's death.

"He's probably just camping out in an old dun. He'll be back soon enough, when his hunger drives him home," I said, not believing the words as I spoke them.

"God grant you the right of it," Rhoderick replied, "but your aunt is aye worried over it all, and your uncle too, although he says less. And he himself was asking me to sail over and fetch you, for he was saying there is none like you to be finding something lost. Or someone, as it would be."

"When was the boy last seen?" I asked.

"Two days ago it was. He went with his foster-brother Dòmhnall up to near the Tràigh Bàn, to look for that red cow that had wandered away from near Beinn Beag, but then he and Dòmhnall were quarreling over something and Dòmhnall left him there. And he never came home."

"Could he have taken a boat out?"

Rhoderick shook his head. "There are no boats missing. And the boys were walking to the Tràigh Bàn."

"Well, I had better be coming with you then." I looked at the sky, where the sun was just disappearing. A shaft of light streamed out through a break in the now purple clouds, turning all I saw to molten gold.

"Were they sending word to Finlaggan about it all?" I asked.

Rhoderick shook his head. "Your uncle has sent a man to Benbecula, to tell the boy's parents. But I am thinking he is hoping the lad will turn up before he is having to tell his grand-father."

"Well, we had best be on our way and looking for him, then," I said, with more confidence than I was feeling. "It is late to be sailing tonight, though."

"And the crew is tired," put in Rhoderick.

"Tomorrow morning? Will that suit? Come in and rest."

I turned to Alsoon, who had already sent her husband to gather some extra bracken for beds. "Alsoon, prepare for these visitors. It will not be fancy, but I can promise you men full stomachs tonight and a dry place for sleeping. We leave at first light tomorrow."

The next day dawned fair and bright, and we set off early in the small *birlinn* Rhoderick had brought from Colonsay. I had not intended to bring my dog, but the hound whined so as we boarded that at the last minute I brought him with us. The crossing went swiftly, and it was soon enough that we beached the boat on the small cove at Scalasaig. I left the harbor and started the climb up the hill to Dun Evin, my uncle's home, with Somerled by my side, as I had so many times before.

Gillespic, my uncle, was chief of the Clan MacPhee. Dun Evin was his home, a fine fort overlooking the town of Scalasaig on the Isle of Colonsay which was all the territory we MacPhees had to our names. A fine enough island it was, for all that it was not overlarge. Advocates at the Court might argue that we held the land through the grant of King Robert Steward to the Lord of the Isles, and from him to my uncle, the chief of our small clan. But whatever they might say, we who lived on Colonsay knew that the MacPhees had held the island back to the time when Celt and the Norse vied for control of this land. The king in Edinburgh could think what he wished about it all.

I turned at the entrance to the dun, taking the moment to rest my bad leg. As a young child I had caught the fever, and after that my right leg had grown weak and crooked, causing me to limp. After the steep climb up the hill to the fort, the muscles of my leg pained me.

I gazed down on the little port of Scalasaig, the harbor, and the sound. Farther away across the water, the Paps of Jura rose out of the bulk of that island, and a bit further to the southeast lay Islay. It was a fine day for October, the sun shone brightly on the water and Colonsay looked green and gentle to my eyes. Too gentle for such sad happenings as lost young boys. I squared my shoulders, turned back, and greeted the guards at the entrance to the dun. They smiled to see me and Somerled, then let me pass, and I entered my uncle's fortress.

Somerled immediately started barking at my uncle's hounds, who bayed back, starting a ruckus. There was a frenzy of howling and the courtyard became a maelstrom of dogs, jumping and sniffing at each other.

Uncle Gillespic stood in the forecourt, looking solemn, covered with mud and dirt. He had been speaking with some of his *luchd-tighe,* but broke the conversation off at the noise of the dogs. "Stop that," he yelled, but the dogs ignored him. Perhaps they did not hear him for all the noise they were making. My uncle's hazel eyes brightened a bit when he saw me, lightening the tension in his face.

"And here is Muirteach. And you were bringing your dog as well. We shall see what you are thinking of it all."

I embraced my uncle, who gripped my shoulders hard a moment before he let go. It had been some months since I had seen him, and I realized how I had missed him. Somerled nosed around my uncle and me, adding to the general confusion.

"You are looking fine, Muirteach. You've put on some weight. Sure, it must be that Islay is agreeing with you these days. You are not missing your house in Scalasaig?"

"Well, I am not missing the leaky roof," I hedged. "But what has happened?"

Gillespic's eyes darkened. "Niall and Dòmhnall went off to the Beinn Beag, to bring some of the cattle back from pasture, and that red cow had wandered off. That one is always wanting to go up to the shielings whenever she is getting the chance. But then Niall had some fey idea about looking for faerie gold up there. He was saying he had found some on the rocks nearby."

That did not sound so dire to me, like many a boys' expedition. I said so, although most boys were quick enough to return to the dun when they got hungry. And Niall had been missing for three days now.

"Och, yes. But then Dòmhnall was thinking it might not be such a fine thing to be doing, he was feared the *sithichean* would be angered and come and take them away over it all. I am telling you, Muirteach, I will be sending that boy to the priory. I do not think he will be making a chief, not that one."

"Aye." I agreed, thinking of my young cousin, dark-haired like myself, and studious. "Dòmhnall will be liking it there, I am thinking. He does not seem to be much of a boy for adventure. He will make a fine priest. A better one than I did." I had spent time at the nearby priory as a youth, but had left there while in my teens. I had no wish to be a monk, but it might suit Dòmhnall well.

"But what of Niall?" I continued.

"Well, Dòmhnall left him. Which is fine enough. Niall knows the island well, for all that he is not old. He has been here for two years. But he did not come home. That was three days ago, and we have not seen him yet."

"And you've searched for him?"

"Fergus and Seamus have been combing the hills and the caves as well. They've found nothing. And I was clambering in and out of the caves by the Tràigh Bàn all day. As you can see." My uncle gestured to his muddy clothes.

"And what does Dòmhnall say of it all?"

"Just that he left him there, up near the Carnan Eoin, that big hill that overlooks the beach."

"They could have squabbled. You know what boys are like. You raised me, after all. Perhaps Niall is hiding to get Dòmhnall in trouble."

My uncle looked grave. "I am not thinking so, Muirteach, and neither are you." I nodded. "Well, let's away in then, and be speaking with your aunt about it all."

Aunt Euluasaid was in the kitchen, seeing to a roasting side of venison. Although her coif was as white and neat as ever, I could see the redness in her eyes and I guessed it had not come from the smoke from the fire.

"Muirteach!" She gave me a warm embrace. As I held her I could feel her start to cry again.

"There now, Auntie," I said awkwardly. "We will be finding him." Surely we would find him, lost in the hills or hiding out at Dùnan nan Nighean, playing soldier.

"Aye." She broke away and dabbed at her eyes with her apron. "I am praying you will, Muirteach, for you are a wise one. I am just praying you will not be finding him too late."

Of a sudden the memory of my dream sprang to my mind again, the funeral procession, the torches. I shuddered involuntarily, then hoped my aunt had not noticed the movement.

If she did, she did not remark on it.

"But, Muirteach," my aunt continued, "here you are just off the boat and you have not eaten. Is it hungry you are? Elidh," she called to one of the women, "just be getting some of those fresh oatcakes and some of that meat for Muirteach, something just to tide you over until the meal that will be coming."

Somerled loitered near the door, hopefully eyeing the roasting meat. "And Muirteach," my aunt added, "get that dog out of my kitchen."

I shooed him back out to the courtyard while Elidh brought the food, then ate hungrily while my aunt told me what little she knew.

"The young *amadan* was speaking of the *sithichean*, more and more often he spoke of them," she said. "He was forever wanting to go over to Oronsay, and the hollow hills that are there. I was warning him against it, and Dòmhnall says he warned him too, and I am thinking that he did. For all that my Dòmhnall is not a brave one, he does not lie." She paused and looked at me a moment, and I was glad to see a faint smile on her face. "He minds me of you, Muirteach, especially now that he is growing older. You have the same gray eyes as my son."

"And so what was Niall doing there?" I changed the topic back to the missing boy.

"He wanted to dig them up. The faerie hills. Niall swore they were filled with gold, and he seemed to have no fear of the *sithichean*. And he was forever bringing things back with him, even when we sent him to watch the cattle. There near Beinn Beag. A faerie arrow he found, one time. And something else."

"What was that, Auntie?"

"Have you finished? No? Well, just a moment and I will be getting it for you, then."

I crammed the rest of the oatcake in my mouth and gulped the last of my ale. "It's fine, Aunt. I've finished. And your oatcakes are as fine as ever they were."

Aunt Euluasaid barely acknowledged the compliment, which told me how worried she was.

I followed her out of the kitchen and into the hall, then behind a partition at the back of the room to the chamber she shared with my uncle. A shaft of sunlight from a small window dimly illuminated the room. She took from behind the bed a small whalebone casket, richly carved with an interlacing design, opened it and removed something.

"Look, Muirteach," she said, holding out her hand.

I saw a gold ring lying on her palm. The beam of sunlight caught it and played with it a moment, sending glimmers through the darkness. A small enough thing it was, a sheet of gold curved and shaped as a rounded disc, with a narrow opening in the center of the piece. Smaller wires of gold wrapped around it to make a ring shape.

"*Dia*," I murmured. "Faerie gold."

Euluasaid shrugged, and returned it to the casket. "Dòmhnall said Niall was bringing it back one day from the Tràigh Bàn; Niall had found it on one of the hills near Beinn Beag. And when Dòmhnall found it after Niall disappeared, he did not know what to do with it, and hid it. But then he was thinking better of it and was bringing it to me. Oh, Muirteach," she cried, breaking down again, "the *sithichean* have stolen the lad! For he had taken their gold." I felt the hairs on my neck prickle and rise and a chill spread down my back at her voice.

"I am thinking it is someone else's gold," I replied, with more confidence than I felt. "But we will find him. Do not worry, we will find him."

CHAPTER 2

I walked with my aunt back to the kitchens, and then I went to find Uncle Gillespic.

"So where have you searched?" I asked him.

"We've asked with the monks at the priory, we've searched the caves near the beaches, we've asked at every cottage on that side of the island. I sent Fergus up to Dùnan nan Nighean, to see if he had gone to ground there. We even checked at Cill Chaitrìona. I had twenty men out searching for him yesterday, after I sent Rhoderick for you. Nothing. He's vanished clean away."

"Euluasaid thinks the *sithichean* have him," I said, and then I told him of the piece of gold.

Gillespic spat and balefully eyed the sun, which was starting to descend in the western sky, as if it was to blame for his missing foster-son. "Aye, she was telling me something of the sort." He spat again, as if he had a bitter taste in his mouth, and turned away from the sun.

"Where is Dòmhnall? And Malcolm?"

"They are out searching for him still. As was I, until just before you arrived here."

The sun was starting to set. It grew dark somewhat earlier these days in October, and the air felt chill. "Are you wanting to go out again today?"

"Muirteach, I am not knowing where to look. That is why I was sending Rhoderick over for you. I am hoping you can help

31

us—you must."

"I will do what I can. Surely a lad can not disappear into the air. He must be someplace."

"Aye, I am hoping so. He is a good lad, for all that he is so wild."

"Have there been visitors here lately?" That last was a foolish question, for always there was someone visiting at my uncle's dun.

"Just Lachlan's second cousin Liam, from Mull. He left two days ago, although he is to return soon. He acts as Lachlan's messenger-boy when he is needing one. And some MacRuaris from Uist. Griogair and Raghnall, they are called. They came on business from the Gorrie there at Lochboisdale. He has a daughter he is wanting to marry to Malcolm. They are still here. I am thinking that Raghnall has met a woman he likes down in Scalasaig, and he is not wanting to return to Uist too quickly."

I had noticed the two strangers sitting by my uncle's hearth when I had entered the hall. "They are knowing the boy's father," Gillespic continued. "But they were helping us look all yesterday and were with me the days before that."

"Could he have gone into the sea for a swim? Perhaps he drowned?"

"It was not that warm that day. And I am not certain the lad knows how to swim, for all that he is a good sailor."

True enough that was. The sea was cold in October. And most island men do not swim, as Seamus and I had discovered that summer to our misfortune, when our boat had gone down.

"Well, I shall talk to Malcolm and Dòmhnall when they return. Perhaps he showed them where he found the gold, and they know more of it."

It was soon enough that Gillespic's two sons returned, dispirited, to the dun.

"And no one has seen anything of him?"

Malcolm, the older, shook his head, his mouth full of oatcake. "No, cousin. Not a sign of him."

"Nor noticed anything unusual?"

Malcolm chewed more slowly. "I am thinking one old woman who is living up there by the beach was talking of seeing someone out on the sands. It was one of the nuns she complained of seeing. From the nunnery up by Balnahard," he added helpfully, before reaching for another oatcake.

"What woman was that?" I asked.

"It was old Àine, the one living near the caves there. On the south side of the Tràigh Bàn, overlooking the beach. Fergus's aunt. But she is so old, you can not always be believing what she is saying."

"Muirteach, can you not go and speak with her?" my aunt pleaded. "Perhaps she was seeing Niall, and was then forgetting it."

The torch flared up a moment.

"Aye, Auntie," I replied. "I'll go and speak with her. Tomorrow."

"Take Fergus with you," added my uncle. "And good horses. You'll make better time that way."

I took a *mether* of ale and sat down next to the two strangers near the warmth of the fire. "So you are from Uist?" I asked.

The tall one nodded. "I am called Griogair, and this is Raghnall."

"I am Muirteach. I am nephew to the MacPhee."

"Yes," said Griogair, his smile lightening his lean features. "We were hearing of you. It was you that found that madman last summer, on Islay. It was the talk of all the Isles."

I nodded, a little embarrassed. "Luck was with me on that day." I changed the subject. "That Niall who is missing is from Uist. Were you knowing him there?"

He nodded. "He is from Benbecula, not Uist," Griogair corrected me. "We are knowing his father, Ranald, who is son to His Lordship. He has lands in Benbecula."

"It is a strange thing," I said. "For a boy to disappear like that."

"Aye," replied the shorter of the men with a scowl, then he returned to his ale.

"Are you knowing the boy well?" I persisted.

"I am knowing the boy's father," Raghnall finally said, still scowling at his ale. "And I have seen his son a time or two since I have been here. That is all."

"Would anyone be wanting to harm the boy that you can think of?"

"Surely no one on Colonsay. The family is from Benbecula, and kin to the MacDonald himself. No one would be wanting to bring his wrath down on them. And he's just a lad, after all. No. He has vanished. We have searched for him. The *sithichean* have him, and that is that." He spat on his hand and crossed himself.

I slept badly, although I did not remember my dreams, but I tried to put a hopeful face towards the task of finding the boy as we set out the next morning just at sunrise. Dòmhnall insisted on coming with us, and as he had been the last to see his foster brother, it seemed wise to me to take him. With the horses my uncle gave us we made good enough time and so it was still early in the day when we reached the Tràigh Bàn and Àine's dwelling. It stood a little way off from some other huts, which belonged to Fergus's parents and his brothers, and looked northward over the fine golden expanse of the beach. Even on a dull and cloudy day such as that morning, with a bit of rain falling and a cold wind blowing the leaves off the rowan tree that stood by Àine's cottage, the sight was impressive.

"Where did you leave Niall?" I asked Dòmhnall, who had come with Fergus and me.

"Just over there." He pointed towards Beinn Beag. "We had gathered the cattle and were coming back. We had not found that red cow that is forever going off on her own, when Niall stopped and picked something up from the ground. Then he was saying he would just be staying a bit longer there and would not be coming back with me. He wanted to go dig, up by that old cairn. I followed him and warned him of the *sithichean*, but he would not listen to me."

A quaver in his voice stopped his speaking for a moment.

"It is not your fault, Dòmhnall," I said, putting my hand awkwardly on his shoulder, wishing I knew how to help him.

"Aye, it is so," continued the boy. "I am the older, and I should have stopped him." He bit his lip, to stop its trembling, I guessed.

"You know how headstrong your foster brother can be. I doubt you could have stopped him," I said, and hoped I sounded convincing. "But perhaps later you can be showing me exactly where you left him. For now, let us be speaking with Fergus's aunt again. Perhaps she will have thought of more to tell us."

We traveled down the track leading to Àine's house. The old woman heard the noise of our approach above the wind, and came outside to meet us as we dismounted. She was an old wizened thing, nearly bent double with the crooked back that age gives to some women, and her brown eyes, when she looked up towards us, had a look of confusion and suspicion in them.

Fergus greeted his aunt and she invited us inside and gave us some fresh milk.

"Now what is it you are wanting?" she asked abruptly after the preliminaries were concluded. "For this young one was here yesterday with his brother. I was telling him already I did not see the boy."

"But were you seeing anything at all out of the ordinary?" I asked.

"There is a lot to see on the sands, out there," Àine replied. "People come and go, like the tides."

"What sorts of people?"

"The folk from hereabouts, mainly. And people come to visit Columcille's well on the other side of the beach there, in the rocks. Not just Colonsay folk. Sometimes you will see a boat beached there, and then I am knowing someone is visiting the well from another island."

"And do you see other boats as well? Colonsay men?"

"Just those of his brother," she said, nodding towards Fergus.

"So you were not seeing the young boy?"

"Wasn't I just saying as much?" she retorted, sounding annoyed.

"I know, Granny. But surely many others come to the beach here. What of them?"

"The young girls will be gathering seaweed. And shellfish. And the men will be coming in from the fishing. The women gather herbs on the hills over there," she added, motioning to the hills above the beach.

"Anyone else? Anyone out of the ordinary?"

The old woman made a sign of protection. "I have been seeing lights on the beach. And on the hills. But that is the faerie, for it is late in the night."

"It could not be people you are seeing?"

She shook her head resolutely. "It is the faerie," she said flatly. "They come down from the hills, from Beinn Beag, and they dance on the beach. I have heard them, have heard their singing. I have glimpsed them there in the hills, as well. And they have taken that boy with them, back to the faerie hills."

We left her house and traveled towards the village at Balnahard, stopping at each house we saw to inquire again for Niall. No one had seen him, although one man remembered seeing the red cow the boys had looked for, and another woman had seen the boys crossing the beach the day that Niall had disappeared.

We searched near Beinn Beag. Dòmhnall showed me the spot where Niall had stopped to pick something up from the ground, in the little valley between Beinn Beag and Carnan Eoin. There was no Niall there, and no sign of him. Then we walked farther up a little crest in that valley to the spot where Dòmhnall had left Niall digging at the stones. We could see a little disturbed section where the boy had been digging, but there was no sign of the boy. The stones looked as they always did, sitting undisturbed, and if they had seen where the boy had gone, they did not speak to us that day.

By now midday approached, and we hurried on towards Cill Chaitrìona. Although not as large as the nunnery on Iona, Cill Chaitrìona had been founded many years past by Beatrice, the sainted sister of Somerled who had founded the MacDonald clan. I had named my dog for him.

Women from all of the Isles came to the little nunnery on Colonsay to take their vows. A stone fence encircled the little stone chapel and the simple cottages where the nuns dwelled, while a cross, old and simply carved, stood near the entrance. We asked the sister at the gate leave to speak with the abbess.

Abbess Brìde, when she came to meet us, was a woman of middle years with an efficient demeanor. She did not invite us in to sit down nor offer us any refreshment, but kept us standing at the gate. We explained why we were here and asked her if any of her sisters had seen anything.

"We rarely leave the nunnery," she replied. "Some of the young novices will be seeing to the sheep and the two cows, but the animals do not stray down in that direction. Sister Euphemia might go that way when she is collecting herbs. And Sister Morag, who accompanies her. They have not been out much lately, what with the weather so wet as it's been. So no one will have seen anything. But I shall ask all the same."

"Might we speak with them ourselves?" I asked.

Abbess Bride looked somewhat annoyed. "There is no need. I am sure Sister Euphemia would have told me had she seen anything amiss."

"But perhaps something little she saw might give us some clue," I begged. "The boy has vanished without a trace. People are saying ungodly things about his disappearance, saying he was stolen by the *sithichean.*"

The abbess crossed herself.

"They are even saying the faeries have been dancing on the Tràigh Bàn," I continued, pressing the point home. "Ungodly rumors will fly about this place. The talk is flying already, I am thinking. You know how people like to gossip. You can see that we must find the boy."

"Yes, I can see that." The abbess bit her lip a moment while she thought. "Very well," she agreed after a moment. "I will send for Sister Euphemia and Sister Morag. Here," she continued grudgingly. "You may come into the chapter hall and speak with them there. We are a small house and have few visitors."

We followed her into a small stone building with some wooden benches within. One of the whitewashed walls was painted with a scene of Saint Catherine tied to her wheel, while Christ looked over the scene from a cross. The room was cold, with no fire, and we were not offered food or drink. I wrapped my *brat* more warmly around me and tried to smile encouragingly at Dòmhnall. We sat and waited in the chill while the abbess went to fetch Sister Euphemia and Sister Morag.

The two sisters came in, eyes downcast, and sat waiting for

my questions. Sister Euphemia looked old and dour. She answered most of our questions while Sister Morag, younger and more demure, said little. Yes, they had left the nunnery last week to gather herbs, as it turned out, on the day Niall went missing. It was the root of the *copag,* or dock, that they had been digging; it grew well on the hills there. They used it for poultices. No, they had not seen a young boy alone, a red cow, or anything else out of the ordinary that day. They went out often, and that day they had been up in the hills, looking for the *copag.*

Eventually, we took our leave. But wherever we went on the northern part of the island, it was the same. No one had seen anything. The afternoon wore on, and finally, frustrated and hungry, we made our way back to the dun.

Chapter 3

A galley had arrived that day from Mull, bringing Liam Mac-Lean back with another message for my uncle from Liam's second cousin and clan chief Lachlan Lubanach. I took an instant and irrational dislike to the man, for some reason I did not fully understand. He was a fine-looking figure of a man, close to six foot, with broad shoulders and a face I am sure most women would account handsome. Blue-eyed and blond-haired, he wore his hair long, walked with a bit of a swagger, and looked every inch a chieftain, for all that he was no such thing. His *brat* was of a fine weave, and he had a fine silver brooch to pin it as well.

He had not heard of young Niall's disappearance, but his expression grew most distressed when my uncle told him of it over a *mether* of ale.

"I am right sorry to hear of this." He turned and sought out young Dòmhnall, as we had just entered the hall. "It's sorry I am to think that my foolish talk could have been to blame for the lad's disappearance."

"And what foolish talk are you speaking of?" asked my uncle, instantly suspicious. "What was he speaking of to you?" he asked Dòmhnall.

"I was just amusing the lads with tales of the *sithichean*, and of their gold," interjected Liam, with a concerned look. "Little did I think the young *amadans* would be taking my words so seriously."

"And what were you telling them of the *sithichean?*" asked my uncle, like a hound on the trail of a deer.

"I can not be remembering all of it," replied Liam with candor. "Can you, lad?" he asked, turning to Dòmhnall.

"You were speaking of that man in Antrim who found the gold in the faerie hills, and came back to find his village gone, and a hundred years gone by. And of the riches that were found in the faerie hills. And you spoke of the *glaiseraig,* and the *gruagach,* but we had heard of them before—who has not known of them on this island? And then we were telling him of the *Tom na Saighid,* the Bush of the Faerie Arrow, over near to Garvard," Dòmhnall added, turning towards his father. "And wasn't it just that Niall had to go there and look for the arrows. But we were not finding any there."

"Indeed," interjected Liam smoothly. "Tales such as the boys might hear anywhere. And as the boy says, they had heard most of the tales before. I meant no harm by it all. And now just look at this coil.

"But where can the boy have gone to?" he continued. "Surely no one on this island would want to do him harm, and it is not such a large island as all that, to hide on. Now on Mull there would be places aplenty."

"Is that a fact?" muttered my uncle, with a dark look on him and an angry glint in his hazel eyes. "Well, perhaps if you will be here for a few days, eating our food and riding our horses, you can be helping us search a bit and you may be finding what we have not yet found, on this tiny island of ours."

"I meant nothing by that, you understand," said Liam, who realized, too late, his slur. "Colonsay is a fine place indeed. Why, my own mother's mother was from this island. That is why I am liking to come here, just, when my chief needs a man here."

41

And so that matter, at least, was mentioned no more.

My uncle was true to his word, however, and sent Liam out with us to scour the island again. We concentrated on the area near the Beinn Beag where the shielings were, the summer pastures, and where Dòmhnall had last seen Niall. Amid a jumble of fallen stones we saw the more recent remains of an abandoned hut, but it looked as if no one had lived there for many years. We continued looking on the slopes of Carnan Eoin, the highest hill on the island. From the top we had a fine view of the island, and the surrounding seas, but no sight of Niall.

Liam MacLean was quite a talker, and with a fine sense of his own self-importance as well. At least so it seemed to me. I grew weary of listening to his tales of the fine cities he had visited—Edinburgh, Aberdeen, and even York on some business of his chief's. Although, I thought to myself, I would enjoy seeing such places myself someday. But not with Liam as a travelling companion.

My mind wandered and I thought of the stories he had told the boys. The *glaiseraig,* the gray slinking one, was said to have once been a woman, enchanted and stolen by the faerie until she was close to becoming one herself. I had never seen her, but Aorig claimed to have seen her one evening, in a gully over by Machrins. A tiny woman, gray-complected, with long yellow hair and a green dress. And sure enough it was that whenever the milking was done, each day in the evening, the milk maids poured out some milk for her on the stones to ensure the cattle came to no harm. For if annoyed, she could be mischievous.

The *gruagach* was her male companion, and it was himself that had been tied up so tightly on Clach na Gruagach near Balnahard that the rope had been leaving marks on the stone. You can see them to this very day. But neither of these creatures was known to steal young boys away.

Although other *sithichean* did. There were many tales of children, and old folk as well, stolen by the faerie. They usually left a changeling behind, with the same look as the stolen human, but some defect of speech or body. And changelings were most often treated well, to ensure the human child in turn was well treated by the faerie in the *sithean*. But there had been no changeling left in place of Niall; he had been spirited away entirely.

We stopped to question an old man living near Balnahard, who showed us another stone near the nunnery where milk was left for the *glaiserig*, and some marks in the stone he claimed were footprints of faerie cows. But there were no footprints of eight-year-old boys to be seen, and he himself knew nothing of the boy.

Near Cill Chaitrìona we passed Sister Euphemia and her assistant returning to the nunnery with baskets full of dock roots. Apparently they had not gathered enough the day that Niall went missing; over a week ago it was now.

It was shortly after that that Liam left us to go after a rabbit he had seen.

"Your aunt will be glad of it for her stewpot, and I'm thinking we'll find nothing more of the boy today." He rode off. I let him go with some relief, shared, I think, by Fergus.

There are several caves along the coast near the Tràigh Bàn, many of them large. Although Fergus said they had searched them, I resolved to look again. It is just the kind of place an adventurous boy would like to explore, as I knew, having been a boy myself on this island.

I decided to start with the large cave on the south side of the beach, despite the lateness of the day. We tethered the horses out of wind and found the entrance to the cave among the rocks of the cliff face.

We lit the torches we had brought with us and the resinous flames flickered and filled the air with a smoky scent of burning pine pitch as we worked our way down the entrance to Uamh Ur, the big cave. We had to stoop and wriggle in, but inside the chamber was larger and one could stand upright comfortably. The floor was mostly sandy dirt, mixed with rock and debris, the walls, shale and limestone and other rock, with moisture seeping on the walls. The damp, musty smell of dirt mixed with old seaweed, and something else, perhaps a dead seabird dragged in by a wild fox, filled my nostrils. As my eyes adjusted a little to the dark, I cautiously straightened up and began to look around. The light our torches cast on the dark walls showed no sign of Niall, nor of any other habitation, but the chamber continued back a good thirty paces or so. Carefully I walked on, Dòmhnall close beside me. Behind I could see the light from Fergus's torch.

The main cavern ended some forty paces back, but a branch led off to the left side, and I thrust my torch through the small opening. I found I did not like this place. Here it was darker and our torches cast less light. None of us spoke much, and when I knocked a loose stone with my foot, the clattering echo of it made Dòmhnall, close beside me, start.

I held the torch high as we looked into the smaller back passage. At first I saw nothing, but then I noticed a spot somewhat lighter than the surrounding rock on one side of that small chamber.

I showed it to Fergus. "I'll go in, as I am the smaller. It will be easier for me to get in there." Fergus agreed without much hesitation. I thought he perhaps liked this place as little as I did.

I squeezed through the small opening in the rock with the wet rocks pressing about me in a black embrace, and was glad enough to emerge in the more open darkness of the other chamber, although I could not stand upright here. I reached back through to grasp the torch that Fergus thrust through the opening, then shone it around, looking for the light patch I had seen earlier. I prayed it was just a light patch of rock, but as the torchlight fell on it, I could see it looked like cloth. I crossed the chamber to look closer. Mayhap it was a rag some animal had dragged in.

The flame shone on what looked like an old piece of linen, wrapped around a bundle of something. The bundle had been wedged into a crevice in the rocks. No animal would push something in so tightly or so carefully. A human had done this. Still, it was far too small to be the lad we were seeking.

I reached out and touched it gingerly; it did not budge. I looked closer and saw that a rock had been placed in front of it, keeping it snug in the crevice. Hands trembling, I removed the rock and, with one more tug, the bundle fell from its hiding place and rolled on the rock floor of the cave. The linen unrolled and inside I saw a collection of tiny human bones.

CHAPTER 4

"They are faerie bones—" Fergus hissed when we carefully carried the bundle outside into the afternoon light. I confess it was glad I was to be away from that dark place, to see the sky, gray though it was in that late afternoon, and the gold sands of the beach, and the waves of the sea.

"No, Fergus. I am thinking it was only an infant. Some poor girl in trouble buried her baby here."

"But why go to such lengths to hide it? And whatever shall we be doing with it now?"

"I do not know why they hid it. But I am thinking we should be taking it to a church for proper burial."

And so we re-wrapped the tiny bones. I should say I, for Fergus refused to touch them. We rode with our sad little bundle to the parish church at Kilchattan, that being the closest one, and added a second mystery to our own.

The priest, Father Gillecolm, was concerned when we showed him what was there.

"The poor wee mite. But it can not be buried in hallowed ground, not unbaptized as it is. I shall put it just outside the wall there. That is the best I can be doing for it."

"Father," I asked, for something had just occurred to me. "Could I be asking you a favor? I am thinking if a physician looked at the remains, perhaps he could be telling us something of it. Would it be too much to ask you to keep the poor thing here for another day or two?"

"The whole village will be talking of it the longer it is above the ground," replied the priest, "and I am not sure that that will be a good thing at all. But I will leave it here, in the back room here off the sacristy for a few days, if you are wanting me to do so. It will do no harm. Perhaps someone will come forward who is knowing of the mystery," he added.

"Whoever hid the baby there was not wanting the remains to be found," I countered. "But someone might know something of it."

We returned to Dun Evin that night, and late it was when we got there. The next day I sent a message to Islay asking for the Beaton or his daughter to come to Colonsay, but it was a good week later before I saw Mariota. Autumn squalls had made sailing across the sound too dangerous, and we waited for fair weather and a boat to arrive from the Rinns.

I say we waited, but the days had been busy with activity. Despite the rain, I had searched more caves near the Tràigh Bàn, and felt thoroughly filthy and damp to my marrow with the effort of it. In one we found a rough campsite, an old hearth and some bones of a rabbit and perhaps some birds, but in no cave did we find any trace of Niall. It was indeed as if the faerie had stolen him away.

No one claimed to know anything about the infant bones we had found. But one old man, Eachann Beag, who lived in a little cottage off the track towards Balnahard, claimed to have passed a stranger one evening about a month earlier as he was looking for a lost goat.

"It was near Beinn Beag, right enough," he said. "And the moon was just close to full, and starting to rise, and so it was close to a month ago that it was. I was looking for that Muireal. She is a great one for wandering as high as she can get, and I was thinking she had gone up to Carnan Eoin, for sometimes she is finding grazing there, and I was worried for her. So I was walking that way, and had just passed Beinn Beag, and that old ruined house that is up there, and what should I see coming but a stranger down from the mountain. Indeed he was a stranger."

"Not a Colonsay man?"

Eachann shook his gray head emphatically. I do not know why he was called Beag, for small he was not. Despite his age, Eachann had broad shoulders and was somewhat stout.

"Indeed and he was not," he repeated. "I had never seen him before. He was thick through the shoulders and looked to be strong. I am thinking his hair was red, but in the moonlight it is hard to be knowing for sure. I greeted him pleasantly enough, but he did not answer me and walked past. And then I was thinking perhaps he was not a good man himself, and I let him walk on, just, and went on to look for my goat."

"He was alone?"

Eachann nodded. "And then I watched him, and he went down towards the Tràigh Bàn. I am thinking he had a boat there, and that is how he came here."

"Why is it you are thinking that?" I asked.

"However else would he have come, and no one seen him or known him here?"

Eachann had seen the strange man a good three weeks before Niall had vanished.

"And you have not seen him again?" I asked, hoping he had.

"No. For my Muireal has not strayed again, and so I have not gone out looking for her in the moonlight."

So here was another mystery to add to my growing store of them. I thanked him, but either the old man saw people invisible to everyone else, or the stranger had been very sly. No one else I spoke with claimed to have seen him, not even old Àine, whom I visited again one afternoon when the sun shone and a mild breeze blew in from the sea. As the day was so fine, we sat outside her cottage, and I drank a *mether* of her ale. Somerled settled himself at my feet and slept in the sun while we talked.

I told her of the small skeleton we had found, and asked if she knew of any local girls who had been with child.

"That girl from Loch Fada, who was handfasted to Hamish. She is second cousin to my niece on the other side. She had twin *bairns,* but they are thriving and learning to walk now. And I am thinking that she and Hamish will be married proper in the church very soon. He was away, you see, fighting in Ireland. He has relatives with the Mhic Suibhne, and he was not knowing of it all until he was coming back this summer."

"There are many other other young girls on the island."

"Yes, but they are well behaved."

I doubted that all of them were so well behaved as all that, but if an island girl had been with child and successfully concealed it, and then gone to such lengths to rid herself of the baby, I supposed it was possible no one would know of the pregnancy.

Suddenly old Àine crossed herself. "It will be a changeling, that is what it will be," she said abruptly.

"What are you saying?" Of course I had heard of changelings, but never of one left dead in a cave carefully swaddled in linen.

"When the *sìthichean* take a baby, they will be leaving a changeling. And you can never be feeding it enough. It will be crying and wailing night and day, day and night. And you must put some iron in the cradle to protect the baby, otherwise they will be stealing it away."

I nodded, for I had heard the same myself. The faerie are said to detest iron.

"You must also be seeing the faerie doctor, if you can be finding one. For they will know the ways to get your own child back."

"And who would that be?"

"It will be someone who knows about the faerie, who knows

the charms to say against them and who can find the medicines
to make the *sithichean* give back the child. Old Gillean, he will
be one of them."

"And where does he bide?"

"Over near the Lochan Gammhich. He was getting his skills
from his own mother."

I took another sip of the ale, somewhat puzzled. "But how is
that explaining the bones in the cave, Àine?"

The old woman looked confused. "What bones are you speaking of?"

"The bones I found in the cave, the ones you said were of a
changeling?"

"I was saying no such thing. I was telling you of the *sithichean*," Àine replied, and as she seemed to get more and more
confused the longer we spoke, I drank the last of my ale, roused
Somerled, and took my leave, remembering how Fergus had
complained of her forgetfulness.

Somerled and I walked back to Scalasaig. I wondered about the
girl from Loch Fada, but that did little to solve the question of
what had become of Niall. And it was with great misgiving that
I saw several boats in the harbor, what with the letup of the
squalls and the arrival of better weather. Sure enough, one
birlinn was from Benbecula, and it had carried Niall's father
and mother on it, grieving parents I had no answers for. But I
was much happier to hear another ship had arrived, a small
boat from Islay with Mariota Beaton aboard it.

It seemed Mariota had already disembarked. Upon question-
ing, it turned out she had not gone up to Dun Evin, as might
have been expected, but had gone into Scalasaig to visit Aorig,
whose cottage was next to the dilapidated hut I had lived in
there. I decided to stop by, reasoning that Mariota might want

company on her way to the dun, where I assumed she would be staying.

My old hut, next to Aorig's neat holding, was not looking the better for the neglect I had bestowed upon it these last months. I thought I should be getting someone to live there before the winter set in, but I walked right by the tattered and bedraggled thatch, and knocked on the wall of Aorig's house, hearing feminine voices chattering inside amid the clatter of cooking and the noise of children.

"Ah, it is Muirteach," said Aorig easily, as she answered the door. "And you have your dog with you as well. I was wondering when we might be seeing you both. Is it Seamus you're seeking, then? He is off hunting with his father. I am not expecting them back until tomorrow." Her face grew more serious as she added, "You've found nothing yet, then? I was just telling Mariota of the whole sad business."

She ushered me inside, and sat me down on a stool near the hearth. Three children, the littlest just learning to crawl, played in the cottage. They were my own half brothers and sister, although how they came to be living with Aorig is another tale entirely.

"Perhaps I can be finding you some ale," Aorig said, pretending not to notice when the middle child, Sean, and his older sister came and clambered into my lap with cries of "Muirteach!" The boy was out of my lap just as quickly, and began chasing Somerled around the cottage, knocking over a bench in the process. Aorig quickly told the boy to take my dog outside.

I looked for Mariota and found her sitting on another stool, smiling a little, and I wondered suddenly what she found so laughable about the situation.

"I can see that great dog of yours is doing well. Is it terrorizing the Rinns entirely he is?" asked Aorig, as she handed me the ale. "And why is it you were sending for Mariota?" she continued without giving me time enough to answer the first question.

I explained about the bones we had found in the cave, and how I hoped someone with some healing skill might be able to tell me something of them. Aorig just shook her head, her eyes twinkling.

"I do not know what she could be telling you about those old bones, Muirteach. I am thinking there is some other reason you were sending for her." Her voice had laughter hiding in it. "Perhaps you have not been feeling too well and were wanting a doctor. Is it a sore throat you've got, then?"

Mariota turned unaccountably red at this comment, but fortunately, the baby, whom Mariota had put down on the bed, tumbled down and began to cry, and Aorig's comment was forgotten. At least I hoped it had been.

I had no chance to speak with Mariota privately until I walked with her up the hill to my uncle's dun a little later. The sun was setting and the evening grew chill as we climbed, while Somerled alternately lagged behind, running after rabbits, then caught up with us. Mariota wrapped her mantle more tightly around her. For some reason the silence between us hung heavily in the evening air, at least it felt so to me.

"You must not be minding Aorig," I said to break the silence.

"I was not minding her at all," replied Mariota, and she kept walking.

"Mariota," I added, after another long pause, "it is good to see you again."

"And you as well, Muirteach."

Just about then we reached the entrance to the dun and were admitted by one of my uncle's men.

"My aunt will be glad to see you," I continued, somewhat

awkwardly. "Aorig was as well." Just then Somerled and my uncle's hounds started yapping at each other, and the noise made it difficult to talk.

We walked towards the hall, where the evening meal was in progress. The torches had been lit against the dark of the evening, and from the doorway we could see the firelight of the hearth. As we drew somewhat closer we heard noise, an uproar of voices, somewhat louder than was the usual at my uncle's hall.

We entered, but no one noticed us. All attention was focused on the center of the hall. The two MacRuaris had drawn their daggers, while across the hearth a well-dressed man I did not recognize sprang to his feet. A white-faced woman in tears stood behind him.

The MacRuaris stood as well, and knocked over the trestle table in a clatter of pitchers, *methers,* and food dishes. The women cried out and I saw members of the *luchd-tighe* rush to restrain the three men. Then the dogs began barking again, in earnest, adding to the chaos, and I saw one of them running to the corner with a large leg of mutton.

"What is it?" I shouted to Fergus, above the babble.

"That is young Niall's father, from Benbecula. The son of His Lordship. And he is saying that the others have killed his son."

CHAPTER 5

It took some time for things to quiet down, and by the end of it Niall's father Ranald and the MacRuaris were under guard in two separate outbuildings while my uncle and I tried to piece together what had happened. The wife of the Benbecula Mac-Donald proved helpful in untangling the coil. It seemed that some fifteen years back, her husband had shot Raghnall Mac-Ruari's son in a hunting accident and there had been bad blood ever since then between the two families.

"Indeed and they were saying nothing of it to me," Gillespic said to her. "They were even helping to look for the boy."

"And a fine thing, wouldn't it be," retorted the Benbecula MacDonald's wife, whose name was Sìne. She spoke with a pinched, taut look to her mouth. "The murderers themselves to be helping to look for my poor Niall, and themselves knowing where not to look so as not to be finding him." She burst into tears and my aunt tried to comfort her. "No, no, it's murdered him, they have. And the honor price was paid long ago, and all should be forgotten by now."

Her sobbing took over and I went with Gillespic to speak with the MacRuaris, where my uncle was holding them in the byre.

"We were not telling you of that," said Raghnall bitterly, after my uncle confronted them with Sìne's accusations, "thinking it made no matter, because we were not hurting the young lad."

"And haven't we sat at your table, and eaten your bread and

drunk of your wine," added Griogair, glaring at one of my uncle's tallest and strongest bodyguards who stood, arms crossed, blocking the entrance to the byre. "Are you thinking we are barbarians, then, to be flouting the laws of hospitality in such a way?"

"Although you were out hunting the day the lad disappeared," my uncle said mildly.

"Yes, we were hunting. But not hunting children. We do not quarrel with children."

"No," added the other, a black look on him, "but we will be quarreling with the lad's father, right enough, after this accusation."

"Well, let me just be sorting it out a bit, then," said my uncle placatingly, using the charm he was so noted for. "Fine I am knowing how you helped search for the lad. I am not accusing you of anything. But I can not have you drawing your swords on each other here in my dun. I might need to be keeping your weapons a wee while, just until this is settled."

Grudgingly, the MacRuaris agreed to this proposal, and my uncle went to speak with the MacDonald.

"The men were with me most of the day that Niall disappeared," my uncle said. "But they did go out hunting later in the day."

"And found the quarry they were after—" interposed the MacDonald, darkly.

"Na, na," said my uncle soothingly. "You must not be thinking it was like that. They helped search for the lad, and I have Muirteach looking for him now as well. And you must be knowing how he solved that mystery for His Lordship himself, your own father, in the summer."

"Well, he has not solved this one, has he? But I myself am knowing who the guilty parties are," said the MacDonald. "And my father, your overlord, will be seeing justice is done, if you do not," he added in a threatening tone.

It was a while before my uncle could coax the man Ranald into a less bloodthirsty frame of mind, and later still before I could eat and speak again with Mariota, who was helping my aunt repair the damage caused by the melee in the hall.

"Och, what a mess. What great lummoxes men are, with their fighting and quarreling," said my aunt as she picked up the shards of a broken pitcher and took them out to the midden. It was not the first time she had done so in my uncle's hall.

"What a reception your uncle arranged," said Mariota with a nervous laugh. "Sure, it was quite unexpected."

"You were not hurt?" Something in her tone of voice made me think that she had been.

"No, Muirteach." She bent her head to pick up some wooden bowls that lay scattered on the floor. "No, I am not hurt. It is just that since last summer I find myself unaccountably sensitive. My humors seem unbalanced, but I am not knowing why."

Thinking back to those events on the Oa last June, in which Mariota had nearly lost her life, it did not surprise me altogether that she was skittish now. But the thought of what my stupidity and foolishness had put her through, and how it had affected her, hurt me like an unexpected knife thrust in my gut.

"It's sorry I am about that, *mo chridhe*," I said, surprising both her and myself with the endearment.

"No now," Mariota said in a lighter tone as she saw my face. "It's fine I am, Muirteach. You do not need to be worrying yourself about me. I am thinking we should both be worrying about that Niall. And what is all this you were saying back at Aorig's about bones? Your message was not all that clear."

It had been so long since I had sent the message that I could not remember. "What was I saying then?"

"You asked if either I or my father could come look at some bones. And it was a lucky thing I was not at Balinaby when the messenger arrived, for we have often been in Finlaggan this summer."

"I am knowing that," I said, a little churlishly.

"Muirteach, I was thinking I might be seeing more of you, now that you are living in the Rinns, but my father was needing me at Finlaggan." She hesitated a bit. "And I found I did not want to stay alone at Balinaby."

"Your cousin is there—"

"I know. But there is more activity at Finlaggan."

"I am knowing that," I retorted. "That is why I was so careful to be staying at the Rinns. I was not wanting His Lordship to be finding me." I righted a table that had been kicked to the floor in the fight.

We both laughed and the tone grew easier.

"I am thinking he'd be finding you easily enough, as it was Himself who was giving you the property."

I explained to her about the swaddled bundle of bones we had found in the cave and about Niall's disappearance. "I have looked everywhere, Mariota, and no one can find a trace of him."

"Maybe he is not on the island. Perhaps he was taken someplace."

"Then he could be anyplace," I said darkly, picking up a bench. "We must first be figuring who could have been wanting to harm the lad. Or steal him."

"There are the MacRuaris. And who else was on the island visiting your uncle?"

"Just that Liam MacLean from Mull. But I do not think he would be wanting to hurt an eight-year-old boy he does not know."

"And what have others seen?"

"A man was seeing a stranger near where the boy disappeared, late in the night. He said it was not a Colonsay man.

57

But that was some weeks earlier, and he was not seeing him again."

"But what would a stranger be doing on the island in the middle of the night? Visiting Columcille's well?"

The hall by now was looking more to rights, and Euluasaid was pleasantly surprised when she came in again.

"Eh, that will do fine, I am thinking. Thank you, the both of you. Why, Mariota, it's exhausted you look. Come now, and I will just be getting your bed prepared. And you were not eating, what with those great *amadans* and all their trouble. Muirteach, you will be excusing us then. And you—"

"I'll sleep in the hall, Auntie," I said quickly. "I'll be comfortable enough here, indeed."

"Well, that will be fine then." And with that she ushered Mariota away to her quarters.

I wandered to the kitchens and found some meat and bannocks, and took them back to the hall, and ate. Then I wrapped myself in my *brat* and lay down on two benches pushed together. I watched the smoke from the fire curl upwards towards the thatch and wondered, about Mariota, vanishing boys, and old bones.

The next morning Mariota and I rode back to the church at Kilchattan, and I thanked Father Gillecolm for saving the sad little bundle of bones.

"It is an infant," Mariota said, after we had unwrapped the bones and laid them out on the rough wooden table in the back room. "Very young." She touched the tiny skull gently. "Perhaps just born. See how the bones here have not fused yet. And perhaps it is a bit misshapen, from the birth."

"Have you any idea how long it has been there?"

"A year or so, I would guess. Long enough for the flesh to

decay from the bones. Perhaps two years? It is hard to be saying exactly."

"*Dia,* Mariota, where were you learning all of that?" I asked her after we had given the priest permission to bury the sad remains.

"My father is a great one for studying whatever comes his way. As you should know, for it was His Lordship himself who sent him to you last summer. He shows me, and I remember. I find it interesting, for all that it may be a bit ungodly."

"Well, ungodly or no, it is probably not having anything to do with Niall, then."

"No, I would think not. Just some local girl in trouble."

"But no one remembers any girls with child, nor any mysteriously disappearing *bairns.* Not recently, at any rate."

"What of the nunnery?" Mariota asked. "There are women there, and ones who would not be wanting to be found with child."

I should have thought of that myself, what with all the happenings of the last summer. Just because someone is a religious does not always mean they are chaste. I cursed myself for a fool.

The priest went to get someone to dig the grave, and we waited awkwardly in the main church. Then we followed him outside and watched while Father Gillecolm performed a brief burial service over the tiny pile of bones. Some curious islanders looked on. We said, truthfully enough, that it was some old bones that had been found that we were just giving a Christian burial to. But I was sure there would be talk, especially as the bones were buried outside the wall of the churchyard.

On the road back to Dun Evin, I fancied Mariota looked anxious.

"What is it?" I asked her. "Was it those bones that upset you?"

"Muirteach, I am not sure. It's nothing, a fancy, just."

We rode a little farther, and were making our way round the large outcrop of rocks called Beinn nan Caorach when Mariota broke the silence again.

"Perhaps I could be staying there a few days, Muirteach."

"Where?"

"The nunnery up at Cill Chaitrìona. I could ask permission of the abbess to retreat there for a time, say a week or two. And perhaps I will be learning something that will be of help to you. You can put it out that I was overwrought," Mariota added wryly. "For I seem to be, somewhat, these days. I hardly know myself."

"Is that what you're wanting?" I asked curiously. The thought of Mariota in a nunnery bothered me sorely, even if it was but for a short time.

"You know, Muirteach, I am thinking that it is. It had not occurred to me before, but I think it might be restful there. Perhaps I could discover who might have left the bones in the cave. And some rest and quiet would be nice before I return to Islay."

"Well, that is fine then. If that is what you're wanting."

I did not mean to sound curt with her, but I am afraid I did so, and we spoke but little more as we rode the short distance back to the dun. Mariota explained what she was thinking of doing and, although Euluasaid clucked over it all, my uncle replied that it would be no trouble, as the abbess was in his debt for a number of things and would not dare gainsay him. And so that was that.

The next morning I rode with Mariota up to the north end of the island, with Somerled loping along beside the horses, until we reached the nunnery. I introduced Mariota to the abbess.

"I am wanting a retreat for a few days," Mariota explained.

I also handed her the letter my uncle had had me prepare, requesting that the abbess honor Mariota's request. Abbess Bride agreed. As my uncle had predicted, she was in his debt and could not refuse.

"I will fetch you in two weeks' time," I said, somewhat forlornly I am afraid. Mariota thanked me and, almost before I knew what was happening, Somerled and I rode away alone leading the second horse, with the gate of the nunnery enclosure closed tight against us.

CHAPTER 6

It began spitting rain on my ride back to Dun Evin. I took a different path back, one that led up a little valley near the Lochan Gammhich and passed by an old man working in a field there, near a small cottage. I thought this might be the man old Àine had spoken of, the faerie doctor Gillean, and so I smiled and greeted him. He was short and wizened, but still strong, bent over under a creel of peats he was carrying. He set his burden down with some eagerness when he saw me.

"*Dia dhuit*," he greeted me pleasantly enough. "And what is bringing you to these parts of the island on a day like today, and trailing an extra horse as well? And a great dog like that one?"

I explained I had been up to Balnahard, and he invited me inside and offered me *uisgebeatha*. Somerled wormed his way in as well and plopped down beside the hearth. The warmth of the drink and the old man's peat fire took the bite out of the cold dampness of the day and I began to feel less dreary. It was not as if Mariota was taking vows.

From the doorway to his cottage I noticed Gillean could see Beinn Beag, Carnan Eoin, and even down a ways to the beach. I asked him if he had ever seen the mysterious stranger old Eachann had mentioned.

"No now," he said. "But I've seen faerie lights there in that valley often enough."

"And have you ever seen the *sithichean?*"

He crossed himself and spat. "No, I've never seen them at all. But I have heard them, right enough. It will be late that they are making noise. One night the moon was down, but I had been up with a sick cow and was just going to sleep when I heard a thumping sound from over there. I am thinking they were dancing and it was the sound of their feet I heard."

"Old Àine was saying she saw their lights on the beach."

"I was never seeing any lights." He took a swig of *uisgebeatha.* "Although I have heard them many times since I was a child. My mother was saying they stole me when I was but a young one, but she was getting me back again from them. I had wandered off from the house and was missing for a night, but she knew the charms against the *sithichean.* She said them and found me safe enough the next morning up the valley. But ever since then I can hear them dancing in the night."

The rains drummed on the cottage thatch and I settled my back against the wall, for I could see the rain would not be letting up for a while.

"That is a good tale," I said. "You are not remembering what happened to you that night?"

He shook his head. "I was just a wee boy, barely walking I was, and I do not remember. But my mother was saying when she got me back that I had grown shorter in the night. I am thinking they took some inches away from me before they gave me back."

"You were hearing of the child from the dun who has gone missing?"

"I heard something," the old man replied. "Some of the MacPhee's men came by, looking for the lad, over a week ago it will be now. That was the last I heard of it, for there are not so many people that come by this way. Tell me more of it."

I recounted the story, while Gillean sat by the glowing peats and listened.

"The *sithichean* will have him, then," he said. "That will be the way of it."

"People are saying," I continued, "that you are a faerie doctor."

"I can not help everything that people say," responded Gillean. "But it is true enough that I have helped some people when the faeries had them. It comes from being stolen by them as a *bairn*. And I was getting the charms from my mother before she died. May all the saints be good to her soul now. Here, let us raise a glass to her memory."

We drank, silent for a moment, listening to the rain pouring down outside. Somerled whimpered in his sleep.

"There is another thing," he continued after another drink. "Perhaps I should not be speaking of it though, for it may make them angry, and I am not wanting to do that. But I was not keeping it. I threw it back to them."

"And what was that?" I asked him, and reached for the flask myself.

"It was something of theirs, something I was finding, just. Are you having any iron on you?"

I had my dirk, and the old man took it and held it. "That is the best protection against them, and I am not wanting them to be angry with me about it all, so I am trying not to speak of it at all, at all."

"But surely they will not be coming out today in the rain?"

"Perhaps not." He spat and held the dirk by the blade. "Well, I'll be telling you then, and may all the saints be protecting me if the *sithichean* are abroad on this wet day. I was over by Beinn Beag and I found something of theirs. I picked it up and took it with me here to the house. It was a bonny, bonny thing it was— all glowing and golden it was."

"It was gold?"

"Aye, gold. A golden bracelet. Although I am thinking it

would be too large for a faerie woman to be wearing. Perhaps they are using it for something else altogether."

"And where were you finding this thing?"

"It was over by Beinn Beag, as I just told you. It was early one morning, not too long ago. It was just lying there amid the grass. I can show you the very spot that I found it when the rain is letting up. But I do not be thinking they will have been foolish enough to drop all their treasure when they left."

"And what were you doing with it?"

"Och, I got to worrying for the bad luck of it, and so I threw it in the lochan just over there. I gave it back to them, I did."

"Eh, and so Mariota is off to the nuns at Balnahard," said my aunt when I returned later that afternoon.

"And what were you doing, Muirteach, to drive her away like that?"

"I was doing nothing," I insisted, which made my uncle laugh.

"Indeed, and had you been doing something with her, she would not be wanting to go to the nunnery."

"Hush you, Gillespic, to be speaking of her in such a way. I am ashamed of you. And it's not that you don't have troubles enough to concern you, what with those MacRuaris still moping around here and that MacDonald and his wife as well."

"It's fine I can handle the MacRuaris and that MacDonald. I'm thinking if we can just find the lad, that problem will be solved," retorted Gillespic.

Aunt Euluasaid looked sad at the mention of Niall and crossed herself, while I myself felt guilt that the boy had not yet been found. Between the headache I had from Gillean's *uisgebeatha*, and a strange irritation at the day's events, I felt like a snappish hound and suddenly wished only to be away by myself someplace, where I would be free to sulk.

"Aye. Well, Muirteach, and what are you thinking now?"

I scowled, and drank some more ale. I had arranged to fetch Mariota home two weeks hence. It seemed an eternity away. No doubt the MacDonald would be wanting to comb the island again, going over places we had already scoured fruitlessly.

"Keep searching, I suppose," I answered. "And that Gillean was speaking of the *sithichean* near Beinn Beag. Perhaps I should be looking there again." I told my aunt and uncle more of what the old man had told me.

"It's as I feared. The faerie have taken him," said my aunt, looking distressed when she heard the story. "For it was their gold he was after."

"Euluasaid, if there was gold to be found by the Beinn Beag, it would have been found long ago. I don't think the *sithichean* are so careless with their treasure as to be leaving it out for little boys and old fools to be finding," said my uncle reassuringly.

"Perhaps you've the right of it," agreed my aunt. "But I wish we'd find him."

For myself I was starting to wish, the more time passed, that we would not be finding Niall. For a cold fear gripped my heart that we would not find him alive.

In the days that followed I searched again the area around the Beinn Beag and the Carnan Eoin. I questioned Gillean once more. He remembered seeing the red cow wandering in the area before, but he hadn't seen Niall or Dòmhnall that day, now over two weeks ago, that Dòmhnall had left his foster brother on the Tràigh Bàn. As it turned out, it had been a day or two after that when he had thrown the gold into the lochan. But he had not seen the stranger.

The Benbecula MacDonald was eager to join in the search for his son, and so in the next days we clambered in and out of the same caves I had searched before, scaled the hills to every abandoned dun, and looked down cliffs and into every ravine on the island. We found nothing of Niall. Indeed, it did seem as if he'd been spirited off the earth. Things grew less tense at my uncle's dun, and the MacDonald was given back his sword. At the MacDonald's insistence, a message was sent to Finlaggan asking for some of His Lordship's men to come help with the search. I do not think my uncle was pleased at this, but there was little he could do.

That night at dinner the MacDonald's wife started in on her husband and my uncle, saying that no one had been looking for poor Niall, and now we would never be finding him, for the *sithichean* had him. I felt ill at ease listening to her, the more so because I as yet had found nothing of the boy. I tried not to listen as she repeated her rant, thinking instead of Mariota and what she was most likely doing at the nunnery. That did little to improve my mood.

It seemed others found Sine's speech tiresome, including her husband, who had been at the drink after they had come in from searching for Niall. Of a sudden I heard him cut through her sad monotone with his own loud voice.

"If you are so sure we could be finding him if we just looked hard enough, why don't you go and ask the old witch in Jura? Perhaps she can scry for him and tell us where to be looking next. For we have not found him on this island, and it is not for want of searching."

"What witch is that?" I asked.

My aunt did not know of her, nor did my uncle, but the Uist men had heard of her, and one of them enlightened me.

"There is an old witch woman there," he said as he gnawed the last bits of meat off the tiny bones of a quail. "Sure it will be her they are speaking of. I am surprised you are not knowing of her, being as Colonsay is so close to Jura."

"One can not be knowing everything," I observed.

"Och, that is true enough. She is an odd one and keeps the old ways, I have heard. She lives on the west side of Jura, in a cave. There was a woman from Barra who was visiting her, just, when her man went missing over in Ireland. It was the Mac-Neill's daughter. That it was. She was asking her father to take her over there in a galley, and asking the witch about it all. And for that, perhaps, we people on Uist are knowing of her."

"How did the MacNeill's daughter learn of her?"

"I am not knowing that. But sure enough the woman lives there, if she has not died. And I do not think she has, for it was not that long ago that all this was happening."

"And what of her man—the daughter's man?"

"The scrying was telling the witch that he was lost at sea. And it was a little later that we did get word from Dublin that one of the boats had been lost with Barra men aboard."

We turned our attention back to the others at the table, and it seemed that the idea of visiting the witch woman had appealed to the MacDonald's wife. It must have been the need to be finding her son that impelled her. She again started badgering her husband and my uncle as well, saying that as close to Jura as we were, it would be a sin indeed not to visit the witch, and perhaps she herself could be finding Niall while all these men had failed to. Euluasaid listened intently and spoke to Gillespic, perhaps just to placate the woman, but soon enough it was arranged that the two women would go to Jura the next day, with some of the MacDonald's men from Benbecula to accompany them.

I spoke with my aunt after the hall had cleared, and she suggested I join them.

"That would be a fine thing, Muirteach, to have you come along," my aunt said. "For I am not knowing much of this woman. I have heard rumors there was a witch on Jura, but I am not knowing anyone who has ever seen her. It seems aye ungodly to me, and it makes me nervous. I would not be going, except the poor woman is so distressed. And perhaps we could be discovering something. But you are not afraid of things, Muirteach, and you are knowing something of the island. For myself, I would be happy to have you along with us."

At which point my uncle told me I should go with the women, and that was that. I was not unhappy to be going. I felt I had failed already to find Niall, and what with Mariota up with the nuns, I believed I had failed at other things at well. The frustration gnawing in me craved activity. It would be good to leave Colonsay for a day or so. And so I agreed to go.

We set off the next morning. I left Somerled at Aorig's, and my half brother Sean was delighted to be in charge of the dog for a time. The rain had stopped, and a brisk wind blew in the blue sky to take us across the sound. The Paps of Jura showed across the strait, and it did not take long for the crossing. One of the Benbecula men claimed to know where the witch's home was located, but for all that it was the afternoon before we reached the spot. The October days were short.

"I am thinking it will be just up this way," said the Benbecula man as we beached the boat in a small cove. "There is just this wee bitty path up towards those rocks, and the cave will be up there. Yes," he considered, pointing upwards as we climbed, "there it will be, just there. I am recognizing it well now. That will be her house."

The entrance to the witch's house hid among the rocks, and it was just the faint blue smoke of her fire and the scent of the peats burning that gave away the location of the cave. As we approached, we could see that the smoke came from a cleft in the rock face above and that the entrance to the cave had been fitted with a rough door, which stood ajar.

The door creaked open, and we faced the witch.

She looked to be a bit older than my aunt, but not yet ancient. Her hair, a reddish color going to gray, hung down loosely around her weather-beaten face. She glared suspiciously at us as we stood at her doorstep.

"Who will you be? And what is it that you are wanting, to seek out Gormal so?"

The MacDonald's wife started explaining about her son, how he was lost on Colonsay and how it was feared the *sithichean* had stolen him away.

The woman nodded, cutting off Sine. "And what are you having to pay me with should I scry for you?"

The MacDonald's wife reached into her bag, and pulled out a gold coin. She dropped it in the witch's outstretched hand. Gormal bit on it, then, apparently satisfied, nodded to us.

"Come away in then, and we shall see."

The interior of the cave was surprisingly large, with herbs hung drying from the wall. I found it pleasant enough, for the herbs gave the room a sweet smell. The light was dim, as only daylight from the doorway filtered in and the peat fire cast little light. A rushlight stood in a clay stand on a rough table where two crockery bowls sat on the wooden surface.

"Sit you down." Gormal gestured to two rough wood benches. "I will just be making it ready."

We sat awkwardly, not speaking. Gormal went over to a chest, opened it, and pulled out a piece of cloth embroidered with diverse symbols—animals and birds, all interlaced into a connected design of great beauty. This she placed upon the table. She then returned to the chest and pulled out a silver bowl, battered and beaten, with strange figures embossed upon the outer surface. She began to polish the interior with a piece of woolen cloth, chanting softly to herself as she did so. The polished inner surface of the bowl caught the firelight, gleaming silver in the darkness of the cave. At length she seemed to be satisfied, holding the bowl to catch the glow of the firelight, and put the cloth away.

She reached into a pottery vessel for some herbs, which she threw on the fire. Mariota would have known what they were, I am sure, but Mariota was not with us. A sweetish smell and whiter smoke rose from the embers and mingled with the stronger smell and black smoke of the peats. Gormal picked up the bowl again, reciting another rune as she did so.

The witch walked to the back of the cave, to a small spring that bubbled there filling a small pool with water. She had chosen her home well. Speaking a different chant, she filled the bowl with the spring water and, holding it high up before her, walked solemnly to the table, set the bowl upon the cloth and then sat down before the bowl to scry.

She chanted quietly to herself, head bent down, eyes focused on the water in the bowl. Almost a hum her chant was, like the bees. We said nothing, barely breathing, and watched. I was aware at first of the hardness of the bench, the aching in my bad leg, the closeness of the others who also watched. But after a time that all fell away, and I heard only the noise of the witch's chanting. The chant filled my mind and I could not say how long we sat there.

Of a sudden the woman gave a great cry, and jerked as if a fit was on her. Her arm moved violently, knocking the silver bowl and it fell to the floor, the water running away in little rivulets on the earthen floor. Then the witch lay still, her head slumped on the table.

"What is it?" demanded Sine, crossing to the table and shaking the witch violently by the shoulders. "What is it that you are seeing?"

Gormal opened her eyes, staring at the MacDonald's wife. "Nothing. I was seeing nothing. I am sorry, but the scrying did not work today. Here." She reached into her bag and pulled out the gold coin. "Here," she repeated, holding it out to the Mac-Donald's wife. "Take this back, as I was not successful. The Sight was failing me today. Take it back. I am not wanting your gold."

"But what of my Niall?" wailed Sine. "Were you seeing nothing of him?"

"The Sight failed me. I have told you. I know nothing of your son. Now go."

And there was nothing for it then but to leave the witch's house and make our way down to the cove in the late afternoon while the sun sank, a red ball, in the west.

CHAPTER 7

We passed an unpleasant night, sleeping in the shelter of the boat on that small beach. One of the men managed to bring down a rabbit and the women roasted it on a fire we built on the beach. Along with the food we had brought, it made a supper of sorts. Sine showed little appetite, and her distress made it hard for me to eat my own food with any enjoyment. My aunt insisted there was nothing to the strange witch's outburst, but the MacDonald's wife refused to believe her.

"She was seeing something, I know she was. She was seeing that my son is dead, and she was not wanting to tell me," she repeated over and over as we sailed back to Colonsay the next morning.

"Whist, my lady, she was seeing nothing. Not even a witch can control the Sight," said one of her husband's men. "After all, she was returning your coin to you."

"Aye," said my aunt, trying to comfort the woman, "she was seeing nothing, and so she gave the gold piece back to you."

I could not stand to listen to the woman's lamenting as it made me excruciatingly aware of my own failure to find her son, and it was glad I was when the boat finally reached Scalasaig.

The next morning as I ate my porridge and drank some light ale with my uncle, Aunt Euluasaid burst into the hall, flushed and agitated.

"Muirteach, you must come with me. And you too, Gillespic. Come at once."

We followed her out to the courtyard where a young girl whom I did not know stood barefoot, flushed and out of breath, as if she had been running. She must have been about eleven. Her plaited red hair had come undone somewhat and her *brat* was wrapped tightly around her against the chill of the morning. Shy, she kept her eyes fixed on the ground in front of her but breathed quickly, like a frightened animal.

"This will be Seonag," my aunt said. "She is coming from the village over near the coast, Riasg Buidhe. Tell them, girl," commanded my aunt, fixing her with a look. "This is not a time for shyness. Tell the chief what you know."

"It is another child taken by the *sithichean*. In Riasg Buidhe."

"Another child missing?" I asked.

The girl shook her head violently, then raised astonishingly green eyes to meet mine. When she did speak the words came out all in a rush, as if she could not wait to release the burden they were causing her.

"No, no. The boy is not missing. But the faeries have taken him all the same. It is my sister's *bairn*, just a wee boy, barely eighteen months he has, and so healthy and fine he has always been, not a sickness has he had. But in the night they came. They took him and left a changeling. And the changeling is so weak, not like my nephew at all, he is. He has the fits, and they will not stop. We heard of the other poor boy who was stolen, so we thought to come here. And my sister was sending for the faerie doctor, the one that lives over by Loch Fada, as well. And the priest," she added, almost as an afterthought.

"What did you see?"

"I myself was asleep. The entire house was sleeping, and we heard nothing. But then he was so hot that morning, four days ago it was now, and he would not eat, and then he started with the fits. Horrible they are, and he will not stop. It is not Aidan. It is a changeling. We prayed to all the saints, but he will not stop."

"He could not just be sick? With the fever?"

The girl shook her head obstinately. "No, no. He has been taken by the *sithichean*."

"Well, we must go and see," said my uncle, and I agreed.

We made good time to the village on the east side of the island, where a few blackhouses hugged the hills and faced the Sound of Jura. Some fishing boats were pulled up on the narrow beach between the black rocks. We found the cottage easily enough; a crowd of villagers outside clearly indicated which house it was, even if the girl had not been there to lead us to it. Inside there were more people, closer relatives, crowded around the pile of bracken where a young child lay, white and weak, on his seated mother's lap. It was easy enough to see that this must be Seonag's older sister; she had the same red hair and green eyes, although her eyes were red and bloodshot with worry and tears. As we watched the convulsions started again, and the woman held the *bairn* helplessly while he jerked.

Old Gillean appeared from the crowd of people and moved closer to the child. In his hands he held a wooden bowl, filled with a steaming liquid, and I could see some bits of green herbs floating on the surface.

"Here," he said to the woman. "You must try him with these herbs. If he does not swallow, it is a sign he has been taken by the *sithichean*. Get him to take them, and they will help to drive the changeling away and out from him."

The mother nodded tensely and dribbled some of the liquid into the child's mouth while old Gillean stood nearby, watching intently. The child did not swallow. The fit was on him, and a murmur rustled through the women standing watching, like the wind that rattled the bare branches of the black-barked trees outside the cottage.

Gillean shook his gray head. "They have taken him," he pronounced grimly, and the murmurs of the women rose again. "Now we must be getting him back to you."

He took the bowl back from the woman and fished some of the herbs out of the liquid and placed them in the child's mouth. "He must swallow them. He must swallow them three times," he said. The child's convulsions ceased for minute, and the woman was able to get him to take a bit of the herbs while the old man chanted. "In the name of the Father, the Son, and the Holy Ghost, begone from here. Begone from here, back to the *sithean* where you dwell, and leave Aidan as you found him."

The woman tried again to get her boy to swallow, and a faint movement in his throat indicated success.

Gillean nodded. "One more time. That is all that is needed." But as he spoke, the boy started jerking again in shuddering fits, and the herbs fell out of his mouth, leaving a trail of green on the white of his chin while his mother started moaning.

"Now, woman, stop your crying," said Gillean. "It is a sign they are not wanting to let your son go, but we will be getting him back. For if that cure does not work, I have others I can try."

He took a leather pouch from his satchel and sprinkled salt in three circles around the child, chanting all the while. Then Gillean procured a rough pottery flask from his satchel, uncorked it, and threw some of the liquid on the child. I smelled the sharp odor of rank urine.

"Begone from this child," Gillean repeated. "In the name of the Triune God, begone."

The child continued his convulsions unabated, and the mother raised desperate eyes toward Gillean. Some of the liquid had splashed on her as well and it dripped, untended, down her cheek, mixed with her tears.

"What am I to do? How am I to get my son back, my own healthy boy? This can not be him. He has never been sick a day."

"This is the fifth day since he was taken. If the fairies keep him for nine days, there will be no getting him back. He will be gone, like the poor boy from the dun." The women in the cottage murmured again, and the boy's mother started to wail.

"No now, do not be crying. It will do you no good," continued Gillean. "You must keep giving him the herbs, and if he will not take them try giving them to him in the new milk, for that is pure and will be making them flee out and away from him. But if that has not helped him by the eighth day, then we must be trying something else to drive them away."

With these words Gillean prepared to leave, but first he gave the woman a small piece of iron. "You must keep this on you at all times," he told her. "And I myself will be coming back to see how the *bairn* is doing. But try to get him to take the herbs."

He left the house, and after my uncle spoke to the woman, we did also.

"She is a good woman," he said outside. "And her husband is a fine man. It is a shame this trouble has come to them. But I am thinking that the boy is sick and not gone with the good people."

"Perhaps Mariota could help him when she returns from Cill Chaitrìona."

"Aye," agreed my uncle grimly. "I've no wish for a plague of faerie changelings here." He spat and crossed himself. "I am not liking this at all, Muirteach, not at all."

Another driving rain came and kept us all inside, on each other's nerves. I watched the MacDonald and my uncle playing chess, and listened to the sound of the rain drumming on the thatch, trying not to hear the stifled sobs of the MacDonald's wife where she sat sewing in the corner. The Finlaggan men were gambling near the hearth with my uncle's men and keeping my aunt's maidservants busy bringing them ale.

The Benbecula MacDonald, as well as my uncle and myself, had also been at the drink a bit, what with the lack of diversion and all the bad weather.

"That was my knight you took," observed the MacDonald after my uncle moved his piece. "And it was not a fair move."

"Indeed, it was a fair move. But what of the bishop you took a while back?" countered Gillespic.

"You're a cheat, MacPhee. And a murdering cheat, as well."

My uncle, the temper on him, dashed the chessboard to the floor. The sound of the chessmen clattering fell away, and the monotonous thrumming of the rain on the thatch was all that broke the silence.

The two men faced each other like two dogs with their hair bristling. My uncle's men stood, but did nothing else as yet. Euluasaid and Sine watched tensely from the sidelines, but both knew better, I thought, than to try and intervene when their men had the black humors on them.

But then the MacDonald's wife spoke, and not to ease the situation. "And will you be letting him get away with it all? They have murdered our poor Niall. The light of my eyes he was."

"And what cause would we have to be murdering the lad?" roared my uncle, no longer quiet. "A fine boy he was, not like his father. Or perhaps you are not his true father indeed, for I can not imagine a weasel such as you getting such a son."

"And what are you suggesting?"

"Just what I said."

"Ranald, did you hear?" said Sine to her husband.

"Aye, I did," said the MacDonald grimly, going for his knife.

Euluasaid had alerted the *luchd-tighe,* and they grabbed the

MacDonald before he could complete his lunge at my uncle, who escaped with nothing more that a prick on the arm, and the MacDonald a wee cut on the hand.

My aunt finally spoke.

"Och, and will ye be starting a war, fools that you are. And how will that be finding Niall? No now," she continued as both men started to talk, "you must put up your knives and put aside your quarrels and act like Christian souls." And with that she called for food to be brought in.

My uncle and the MacDonald looked at each other a little sheepishly.

"It's overwrought you both are," continued Euluasaid.

"Hush you," the MacDonald said to his wife, who had opened her mouth to speak from her spot by the fire.

"Fine you know we've been looking for the lad night and day. Look, you have both blooded the other. Let you mingle blood and swear as brothers to friendship."

My uncle did not wish to sound henpecked and said, "Aye, my wife has the right of it. A fine Christian woman she is indeed. Come. Let us swear as brothers. For myself, I have loved and treated Niall as one of my own. Come and swear the blood oath with me."

Grudgingly, the MacDonald assented, despite the wailing of his wife. And so the blood of Gillespic and the Benbecula Mac-Donald was mingled before the *uisgebeatha* was brought out and the meal begun, while the rain drummed ceaselessly on the thatch.

By the second day after this, the rain finally stopped lashing the island. We had heard nothing more of the child at Riasg Buidhe, and I decided to go and check on him. Perhaps he had recovered, I hoped, as I walked across hills still soggy with the rain towards the little village, with Somerled loping along by my side. The sun was shining in a cold blue sky and the last of the leaves had been blasted from the trees by the storm. I hugged my *brat* closer to me and walked faster, for the morning was chill. As I neared the village, I saw a little line of figures walking from the cottages to the chapel and burial grounds, slightly south of the village. The women were wailing and moaning, and as I drew closer I saw them kneel at the edge of the chapel yard, still crying, as a few men carried a small shrouded corpse into the chapel.

We had not heard of any deaths at Dun Evin, but as I neared the group I had a sick foreboding of what might have happened. I approached the group of women and recognized Seonag's sister as the chief mourner of the party, and Seonag herself. Their woolen mantles covered their heads, and they watched the men enter the chapel. The women did not go into the churchyard but knelt there in the cold mud, continuing their lamenting.

"And what is this?" I asked one of the women at the back of the group. "Who is it that has died?"

The woman glanced at me and appeared to recognize me. She had a sharp-featured face and dark hair, beginning to streak with gray. "You will be that nephew of the MacPhee up at Dun Evin?" she asked.

"Yes, and he himself it was sent me to see how the young lad was getting along."

She seemed somewhat satisfied and proceeded to answer my question.

"You can see for yourself. It is that Aidan, the poor *bairn*. The faeries were not giving him back, and he has died."

"Indeed? And how was that happening?"

I saw a shadow cross the woman's face and I fancied her expression grew guarded. "They were not giving him back," she repeated. "The boy died."

"It is sorry I am to be hearing that," I said. Just then the little company came out of the chapel and took the small corpse to a freshly dug grave on the far side of the chapel. The women did not follow but remained where they were.

"We should not even have come this far," the woman said to me. "Women have no place at burials. His mother should have stayed at home, but she would not. No, she must follow him here, and this much was permitted. Poor thing," the woman added. "He was her first child. I have lost four myself. But Aidan was a bonny boy for all that. And none of mine were taken by the *sithichean*."

I guessed the fever, or whatever illness the poor babe had, had killed him. I stayed, watching the burial with the group of women until the men returned to the party, and we made our way to the cottage for some food. As we walked, I recognized one of the men somewhat from my younger days on the island. I think I had seen him at Donald Dubh's and I greeted him.

"This is a sad thing."

"Indeed."

"Did he die of the fits? Was there nothing the healer could do to help?"

"There was no healer. Just that Gillean from the other side of the island, the faerie doctor."

"And he could not save the boy."

The man shook his head.

"He could not. He had tried all the cures, and they did not work. Nothing could drive them out of the poor boy."

It was just then that we reached the cottage and went in. I offered my condolences to the poor woman whose son had been lost and drank a little *uisgebeatha* before I left and returned to Dun Evin in the chill of the early afternoon.

CHAPTER 8

The next morning I set out to visit Gillean, to find out more about the death of the poor child at Riasg Buidhe. I found the old man hard at work piling some dried peats up outside of his cottage. The sun shone weakly in the sky, not enough to pierce the cold that had the island in its grip.

"*Dia dhuit*," he greeted me cheerfully enough. "And how would you be this fine morning?"

"I am well enough," I answered, "unlike that poor boy from Riasg Buidhe. I walked over there yesterday to see how the lad was faring and found his funeral procession."

"Aye, it was a sad thing," agreed Gillean. "I have seen it like that before when the *sithichean* will not let the child go."

"How did the boy die?" I asked. "Was it the fits that took him?"

"No," replied Gillean. "No, it was not."

"Then what happened?"

Gillean turned taciturn. "It's as I said. None of my cures worked, and the boy died. Now if you'll be excusing me, I must get these peats stacked today before we are getting more of the bad weather."

I left him and turned eastward, walking over the hills and towards Riasg Buidhe on the east side of the island. As I walked, I mulled over what he had said and not said, and the words of the mourner yesterday. I reached the village and saw Seonag sitting outside a cottage, listlessly spinning with a drop spindle.

She looked pale, and I could feel the sadness and grief of her heart as she sat there on a rough wooden stool. She raised her green eyes to me, then dropped them as if ashamed to meet my gaze. Or perhaps it was just the shyness that had come over her.

"Seonag, isn't it?" I asked.

"Aye."

"I am Muirteach, from up at the dun."

She nodded. "I remember you," she said softly.

"I'm right sorry about your nephew. I came yesterday, and found his funeral. It is a sad thing."

"I was seeing you there."

"What happened, finally? Was it the fits that took him in the end?"

She shook her head. "No, that was not it." She began to speak more rapidly, as if the words could not come out of her fast enough. "They tried all the cures, the herbs, the fresh milk, even the piss, and he still had the fits. And he was burning hot."

"And he had been sick for some time. Your sister must have been aye worried about him."

"Indeed she was. And then the faerie doctor was saying that he must be put to the fire, or else the *sithichean* would never be giving him back. For it was the eighth day, you see."

I nodded.

"But she did not want to do it. She said, 'No, it will kill him.' But then her husband was saying we had to follow the faerie doctor's advice or we would never be getting poor Aidan back. And after a time, she had to agree to it. For her husband was giving her a big clout over it all."

"So she agreed?"

"She had to, didn't she?" returned Seonag, quite matter-of-factly for a girl so young. "And she was sore worried about poor Aidan."

"And so what happened then?"

"He died."

"Of the fever?"

Her eyes filled with tears again. "He just died. It was a terrible thing to see, and didn't the poor boy wail. It made my blood run cold, the sound of it. I can not get the sound of it out of my ears. But old Gillean said that was just the faerie not wanting to leave. Then, after, he made no sound, and the faerie doctor said that he was dead."

Seonag kept her eyes on the ground for awhile. Then finally, she spoke.

"Gillean was telling my sister that it was only the changeling that had died, and that Aidan is even now feasting in the faerie hills." She lifted her eyes to mine.

"Perhaps that is so," I hedged, not wanting to take any comfort from the girl.

"Aye, that must be the way of it," she continued, "for he can not be dead. Not my sweet little nephew. Surely he is there with the faerie. Perhaps he is the child of some faerie queen even now, sitting in her lap, being fed sweetmeats from a golden tray."

"Perhaps so," I repeated, not wanting to distress the child more. There seemed no need now to speak with Aidan's mother. I had learned what I had come there to discover. I thanked Seonag and left the village and returned to Dun Evin.

I told my uncle what I had discovered. He scowled and spat in the fire. "There's no proof of the faerie doctor's harming the boy, Muirteach, and I'm thinking there is no law to prevent such things. No one has complained to me of it, and what am I to do even if they were. The poor boy is dead, whether of a fever or of the *sithichean* there's no telling."

"But what if it was the faerie doctor that caused the lad's death?"

"Perhaps, but the lad was sick with the fever, and mayhap it was the *sithichean* made him so. It is a sad thing, Muirteach, but children die all the time. I'm thinking the less is said about this, the better it will be." And try as I might, I could not budge my uncle from his judgment on this.

One upshot of the new accord between my uncle and the Benbecula MacDonald was that the constant harping of his wife changed somewhat. She began to insist that the MacRuaris were responsible for her missing son. And so, a few days after that fateful chess game, my uncle called me to his private chamber. My bad leg ached, and we were all of us muddy and sore from scouring the caves yet again, this time with some of the twelve men His Lordship had sent from Islay to help search for his grandson.

"Muirteach, I am not liking to ask you to do this," my uncle began somewhat apologetically. He had a look in his eye that I knew too well. I sighed.

"What is it, Uncle?"

"It will just be those MacRuaris. That woman is going on at me as to how they must have killed young Niall. Now I am not believing a word of it, but it is true enough that there is bad blood between them and the MacDonald."

"Aye, I know of it. And so?"

"Well, I was just thinking that if you were to go to Uist, yourself, you could find out what the truth of the story was."

The incident between the MacRuaris and Niall's father having been over and supposedly done with twelve years ago, I felt the truth of that matter might be in short supply. But my search of Colonsay had so far proved fruitless. Perhaps the MacRuaris, wanting revenge, had been involved in Niall's disappearance. There might be some clue there on Uist, or Benbecula.

"I'll send you with some business for Donal. He's the chief of the MacRuaris who lives there near Howmore. We've men enough here, what with those from Finlaggan. They can keep looking while you are gone to Uist. I pray the weather is fine enough for that, for I am not wanting them hanging about the hall all day drinking up all of your aunt's ale and my *uisge-beatha*. That will just be leading to trouble."

"And what will be the reason for my trip?"

"That Donal has a daughter he is wanting to marry to Malcolm. You can begin to negotiate a dowry. Some cattle, I'm thinking. See what he offers. He's a good man. He can tell you the truth of that incident with the MacRuaris and the Mac-Donald."

So I gathered my things while my uncle readied his galley and some of his men, and the next morning, a fair one for sailing, we set off for Uist.

South Uist is a lovely island, more windswept and flatter than Colonsay, with fine views of the western ocean. I fancied I could see Tir Nan Og in the clouds as the sun set in the west and we made our way to the MacRuari's dun.

The headman of the Uist MacRuaris was an older man, and although his fort near Howmore was to my mind not so fine as Dun Evin, it was good enough. He made us welcome, and after we had broken our fast and drunk some of his ale, asked us our business. I spoke privately with him in a corner of his hall. He had no private withdrawing room, although his hall was fine enough, with elaborately carved rafters under the thatch and a fine raised platform for the MacRuari's table. A great fire burning at the hearth took the chill of the autumn sea from my bones.

I told the MacRuari of my uncle's business having to do with Malcolm's possible betrothal. We discussed dowries. I had seen the MacRuari's daughter in the hall, a pleasant enough looking lass with dark hair and blue eyes, and I thought Malcolm would not be too displeased if the match came to pass. For all I knew, they had never met.

"And then there is this other matter," I continued.

The MacRuari frowned. "Aye, I'd heard something of it. That Benbecula MacDonald's son is missing?"

"Yes, not a sign of him. We've scoured the island."

His frown deepened. "A bad thing that, for the grandson of His Lordship to go vanishing away like that."

I concurred. "You can imagine. That Ranald was off to Finlaggan recently, and His Lordship was sending some men over to Colonsay to help in the search, but nothing has been found. However, we were hearing something of a feud between those men of yours and Ranald, and my uncle was wanting to know the truth of it, that was all."

"And so it was for this he was sending you here."

"He also wanted you to know he feels favorably to the betrothal. When they are of an age for it."

At this Donal's frown changed to a slight smile. "Aye, I've met that Malcolm. I'm thinking he would suit my Marsali well." His eyes narrowed as his thoughts returned to the other matter. "They are good men. It was a long time ago that it happened, and the honor price paid many years since. That should have set things to rights." He paused to take a sip of his ale.

"The MacDonald was out hunting," he continued. "Just newly married and come to Borve, he was, and had come over here to Uist hunting as my guest. It was an unlucky shot that killed young Tomas. But I'm not believing it was intentional.

"That son of Raghnall's was running where he had no business to be. It was in the east of the island, in the hills. And then the MacDonald saw the movement and was thinking it was a swan, let fly with an arrow and caught young Tomas through the heart."

"*Dia—*"

"Aye, Raghnall was fair fit to kill Ranald MacDonald, whether he was His Lordship's son or not. But the honor price was paid, and the MacDonald even went on pilgrimage to Santiago de Compostela in Galicia for his sins. I'm thinking he felt badly enough about it at the time."

"But now his own son has gone missing."

"Indeed. I am not thinking Raghnall would be involved."

"Perhaps not. As you say, it was long ago."

"Although he has a sister nearby. Perhaps you could be asking her about it all."

"And what of the lad's mother?"

"She died some eight years ago, giving birth."

At that the meal was ready, and after we had feasted on wild goose, fresh cod and the MacRuari's good ale, we slept soundly in his hall until the next day.

Next morning I asked the MacRuari if he would show me the spot where the accident had occurred so many years ago. He nodded and we went out hunting, accompanied by some of his men. It did not take too long to reach the spot, for South Uist is a narrow island. There was nothing to be seen there; just the hills and the sky and the clouds shimmering over the sea. But the hunting was fine enough, and we brought down some wild ducks that would make good feasting later.

On the ride back to the hall, I asked the MacRuari where I could find Raghnall's sister and he pointed me towards a track running towards the western side of the island.

"Just down there it is, the only cottage down the track there. You'll find it with no trouble. Are you wanting a man to go with you to show you the way?"

I declined and set off down the track. I found the cottage easily, nestled snug against a hill and looking cozy enough for it. To the west the waves broke against a small beach. There was smoke rising from the smokehole in the thatch, and a dog came out from around the back and started barking at me. A woman heard the racket and come out the door of the cottage, wiping her hands on her skirt. It could only be Raghnall's sister; she looked enough like him to be no one else, short and somewhat stout, with glints of red in her brown hair.

"Dia dhuit," I greeted her.

"And the same to yourself," she returned. She looked at me curiously. "I'm thinking that you are not a man from this island. What is it you are doing here?"

I explained I was from Colonsay and had seen her brother there, and he had asked me to send his greetings to her. She nodded, accepting my story, and invited me to sit and have some ale while I told her the news of her brother.

"And were you hearing the sad tale from Colonsay?"

She had not and was curious and shocked to hear of the disappearance of the Benbecula MacDonald's son.

"And wasn't it just justice to him, although I am not liking to say it." She looked at me and took a swig of her own ale. "After what the man did to my own nephew."

"Aye, I was hearing something of the sort. That the Benbecula MacDonald killed Raghnall's son in a hunting accident."

"Aye. And it wound up costing Raghnall his wife as well."

This I had not heard. "And how was that?"

"She was older, nearly past childbearing. But after their son died, she grew so unhappy, and then so pleased when she found herself breeding again. And she died trying to give birth to that babe. He would have been a fine son, had he lived. But he did not."

"And how was Raghnall taking all of this?" I asked.

She gazed at me, as if pitying my stupidity. Then she relented.

"Well, you are not knowing him so well as all that, are you? My brother took it badly, for he loved his wife dearly."

She shuddered a little. "That was a black night indeed, with his wife lying there dead in her bed, red with her own birthing blood, and the body of the poor infant lying blue at her breast. Raghnall, when he saw his wife lying there, swore that the Mac-Donald was responsible for the death, and he swore dark vengeance on him."

CHAPTER 9

"But that can not be true," I said. "I thought the honor price had been paid for the other death, and it was all long over." If Raghnall had sworn vengeance on Ranald MacDonald, Raghnall might indeed have harmed the MacDonald's son.

"Indeed and so it had been, but Raghnall in his grief took it that his wife would never have so wanted another child if the first boy had lived. And perhaps he was right in that."

I thought of my own mother's death so many years ago. And the events last summer that had left my poor half brothers and half sister orphaned. I could understand grief, although I could not heal it.

"Well, it is a sad story indeed. I am sorry to hear about his troubles, for your brother seems a good man."

"None better. He has a kind heart, as soft as a *bairn*'s for all of his wild talk. And all that was long ago and over now. He is courting another woman, although he has said little of it to me. I am thinking she is from your own island. He did tell me he was hoping she would consent to be married in the spring. I will be glad to see him home again though." A shadow passed over her face. "It is lonely here, and I fear I talk too much to strangers."

With that she stood up abruptly. "You will excuse me now. I am thankful for the news of my brother, but I still have much to do today before the sun sets."

I thanked her for the ale before she re-entered her cottage, and I heard the grinding noise of her quern as I remounted my horse and rode away.

We stayed in Uist another night and the third day made the long sail back to Colonsay. The dun was packed with the extra men His Lordship had sent from Finlaggan, and I found the crowd oppressive. Aunt Euluasaid and her maids were fair put to care for all of them, and I think my aunt was relieved when I took Somerled and went into Scalasaig, sleeping badly in my leaking cottage there.

The day finally came to fetch Mariota from the nuns up at Balnahard, and I was happy to see the sun peeking through the gray clouds a bit. Like a good omen, I hoped, as I prepared the horses to go up that way. I took the track that led over the hills by Bride's well and then down towards Loch Fada and up to Balnahard at the far end of the island. The sun did not abandon me altogether, but the short October day was half gone by the time I arrived at the nunnery.

The same dour-faced sister opened the gate to me.

"I am here to fetch Mariota Beaton," I explained. "The one who's been staying here the while."

As though the nunnery had many women there on retreat. There were probably no more than fifteen sisters in the whole house.

I was left to drum my heels in the courtyard awhile, and eventually Mariota emerged, embraced the dour-faced sister, who actually smiled at her, said her good-byes and turned towards me.

I scanned her face, thinking perhaps that after her days of retreat she would look different, and was relieved to see her eyes just as blue, her hair just as golden. I am not sure what I expected, but my heart jumped a little when I saw her smile at me.

"And so, Muirteach," she said, "you've come to fetch me back."

We spoke little until we had ridden some distance away from the nunnery and were alone among the heather hills. I felt shy, almost as if I did not know her. Too shy, indeed, to be my usual surly self.

We let the horses set their own pace, not a quick one. It was Mariota who got the talk flowing between us again, asking what we had discovered during her time away. I told her of our visit to Gormal, and the trip to Uist. I told her of the wee boy who had died over at Riasg Buidhe. It seemed I had much to tell her. Then, finally, I asked her of her time with the nuns.

"My stay was pleasant enough, Muirteach," she answered. "I helped the two sisters with the herbs and showed them some new remedies they might add to their store. I felt safe there, enclosed by that wall. No one could come in."

I thought grimly to myself as I listened that a community of women was not all that safe, although in fact the times were safer than those of olden days, when the Vikings raided even Iona. And Colonsay, as well. No one raided monasteries and nunneries these days, as she had said. No doubt she was safer there after all.

"I am wondering you were not wanting to stay," I said, "what with feeling so safe there and all. As if all the men of His Lordship could not keep you safe."

"The place was restful enough," she answered, not being drawn by my tone of voice. "Perhaps I will go back someday. There, or to the nunnery at Iona."

We rode on a pace. I could think of no rejoinder and wished I had not asked the question at all.

"Although," Mariota continued after a bit, "all was not total harmony there."

"Indeed?" I asked, steering my horse away from a particularly succulent patch of grass he was showing too much interest in.

"No. Even in the infirmary the two sisters were not getting along all that well. The older one, Sister Euphemia, was always finding fault with Morag. And Morag did not seem to be especially happy helping there. She can barely tell one leaf from another."

"Is that so?" I asked absently. Truth to tell, the less I heard of the sisters, the better it suited me. But Mariota seemed to want to talk of it all, and I did not want to appear unattentive.

"Yes. I am thinking Morag is not all that happy to be among the nuns. She was a younger daughter of a minor chieftain in Mull, and there was little dowry for her. And her father had prayed for a son, which he got off his second wife, and had promised his younger daughter by his first wife to the church if his prayers were heard. And so Morag was sent to Cill Chaitriona."

"How many sisters are there altogether?" I asked, not wanting to hear more of women promised to the church.

"There are thirteen. The abbess is from Islay, from Finlaggan. She is a cousin to His Lordship. And Sister Euphemia is a Colonsay woman. But they are from all over the Isles. There is even a sister there from Harris."

"Indeed?" I asked, wishing I had something else to speak of. Then I remembered she had not heard of my speech with Gillean, and I told her of it.

"Well, there was little talk of the *sithichean* in the convent," Mariota said. "There was not much talk at all, and none of it was of the faerie. Nor of gold."

"However that may be," I said, "this makes two pieces of gold that have been found near the Carnan Eoin. And faerie gold or no, I am thinking people would kill to get it."

It was just at that point that we neared Beinn Beag, and Mariota suggested we stop and look around as the horses needed a rest.

"As if I haven't searched the area before."

"Aye, Muirteach, but two sets of eyes see more than one does. And after my weeks in the convent, I feel I am seeing everything afresh this day."

The rocks there appeared as undisturbed as ever. But it was Mariota who found a few strands of woolen thread caught on an old thistle nearby. And the thread looked to be the color of the plaid that Niall had been wearing by all accounts on the day he disappeared.

The sun went down early so close to Samhain, and although we looked over the area, we found nothing else, and rode back to Dun Evin saying little. My aunt fussed over Mariota and made much of her. The Benbecula MacDonald was well-disposed towards the daughter of the famous healer Fearchar Beaton. His wife, who I was liking less and less, pestered Mariota continually with requests for headache remedies and sedatives and such things, so we had little chance to speak more that evening. In addition, Liam MacLean had returned from Mull on more business from Duart with my uncle.

He sat next to Mariota as we ate and the two conversed, but from where I sat, near the Benbecula MacDonald, I could hear little of what they said. All in all it was a harmonious evening, with no thrown chessboards or drawn swords. Apparently Ranald and my uncle had taken their pledge to heart, and Ranald seemed to have curbed his wife, for she made no wild accusations even after we showed them the threads we had found clinging to the gorse. She simply withdrew to her quarters, where we heard the sound of weeping.

The next day Liam MacLean left the dun early, to go riding, he told Gillespic. He seemed content to go on his own and my uncle, busy with other affairs, let him go. Mariota went down to

Scalasaig to visit with Aorig and the *bairns*. I wrote some letters for my uncle having to do with his business with the MacLean of Duart and somewhat grumpily waited for Mariota to return. While I waited I spoke with my aunt, who was overseeing preparations for the upcoming Samhain—the speckled breads must be baked, and other foods prepared for the feasting. We were interrupted by Rhoderick and some of the other men who had been out hunting. He stooped as he came in the kitchen doorway, for Rhoderick was a tall man, shook off some raindrops, and dropped a great pile of coneys almost literally in my aunt's lap.

"And are you not the grand hunter," smiled my aunt, looking up at him approvingly. "Will you be wanting ale, Rhoderick? Aye, I can see that you will. When have you ever refused it? Why I am bothering to ask you that I do not know," said my aunt as she filled a *mether* with drink and handed it to him. "You had good hunting, I see."

Rhoderick nodded. "We ran into that MacLean from Mull. Over on the north side of the island, he was. What he was doing there, I do not know."

"He was borrowing a horse from the MacPhee and was going out riding. Before even the porridge was ready this morning, he was leaving. It must be he is just keen on riding," my aunt answered. "And the Tràigh Bàn is a beautiful sight, no matter what the weather."

"What was he doing at the Tràigh Bàn?" I asked.

"It was a ways he was from us there. He was walking his horse when I saw him, just. We hailed him. He waved but did not approach us," answered Fergus.

"Doubtless he was intent upon enjoying the view," I said.

My aunt glanced at me. Liam MacLean was all that I was not. Tall, with blond hair and a beard, accounted handsome, I guessed, by most women. He had often been to Colonsay and today, thinking of his good looks, and in particular the attentions he had paid to Mariota at the dinner the night before, put me in a black humor. No doubt a brawny man like himself would make her feel safer than a scrawny cripple.

I myself am not overly tall. My hair is dark and my eyes an unremarkable gray, although for some reason my aunt considered me attractive, and used to tease me about it. I was not in a mood to be teased that evening.

Of course, I told myself sternly, I did not care what Mariota felt. If she wished to flirt with a handsome stranger or shut herself up in a nunnery, it was all the same to me.

"Well, when he returns, Muirteach, you can be asking him why he went riding if it is important to you," Aunt Euluasaid said and handed me my own *mether* of ale with a sympathetic look, which for some reason irritated me the more.

"I'm going out," I said shortly after I had drained the ale. And I rose from my seat in the smoke-filled kitchen and left.

I walked down the hill towards Scalasaig. The sun was already sinking low towards the west. I shivered, for the damp was cold and the early darkness had something not altogether canny to it. As I neared the bottom of the hill, a horse and rider nearly ran me over. He pulled up short to avoid trampling me, and I glared resentfully up at Liam MacLean through the dusk.

"And where is it you're off to, Muirteach?" he called jovially.

"Just down to Scalasaig. And you? Where are you coming from, then?"

"I was just up to the north of the island a bit. It is a fine bit of an island, this Colonsay."

I bristled a little at hearing my home called a "bit of an island." Although truth to tell, Colonsay is much smaller than Mull, or even Islay for that matter.

Liam dismounted and made as if to walk his horse up the hill to the dun.

"I'm off to Donald Dubh's," I offered, surprising myself. "Come with me, then. His wife brews fine ale."

Liam looked surprised, as I was myself at my offering. But he shrugged, and said, "Well enough."

And so we reached the village and the alehouse.

What passed for a tavern in Scalasaig was really a largish house with the ale-pot standing on a pole in front of it. And as Donald's wife was a good brewer, and since Donald himself had made the *uisgebeatha,* the place was often busy, as it was this late afternoon.

The talk died away for a moment as we entered, and folk stared at Liam with interest, although on a small island like ours, most everyone knows who everyone else is, even visitors. We got some ale and some *uisgebeatha,* and settled ourselves on a bench by the fire.

"And what were you finding up to the north?" I asked Liam as the whiskey settled itself in my gut and the afternoon began to seem less onerous. I did not really expect a truthful answer. Nor did I feel I got one.

"I was out for the deer. But saw only a coney, too bedraggled with all the rain it was to hop out of harm's way."

"We have been searching for that Niall since you were last here. You were not seeing anything of him at all?"

Liam smiled almost apologetically. "Not a trace. It is a sad thing, that. No, it is just that I am liking the view from the Tràigh Bàn. It is a lovely little beach, that one. And I enjoy riding."

A man sitting close to us overheard us, and spat and crossed himself. "That is aye foolish of you. You would not be knowing, as you are a stranger here," he interjected, "but Muirteach here should have been telling you of it, for he is an island man."

"And just what is that?" asked Liam with an amused smile.

"The *sithichean.* You would not be wanting to disturb them.

They have been seen in the Tràigh Bàn, and over by the Beinn Beag. Was it not my cousin himself that was seeing them over there, just the month or so past? And they were stealing that poor *amadan*, were they not, Muirteach?" the man added accusingly. "Two children now. The poor *bairn* from Riasg Buidhe and the boy from up at the dun. For you have not been able to find him—no, indeed they have made away with that poor boy altogether." He spat again and drank some more whiskey. "Indeed, I should not be speaking of them at all, not now, so close to Samhain. It is this whiskey that does it. I'm away from here." He started to rise.

Liam laughed. "I've seen no sign of the *sithichean* there. Just a fisherman or two, an old man out chasing his goats, and some women gathering herbs. But perhaps they will not be showing themselves to me as I am a Mull man," he added placatingly as the other man bristled a little. "I thank you for your warning, for it was kindly meant. Here, let me buy you another drink."

This offer was readily accepted, and the man settled himself back in his seat. Still, the talk in the tavern lingered on the topic of the missing Niall, with many backward looks into the shadows, as if the speakers thought to find the *sithichean* themselves sitting there drinking claret or ale among us.

"I was hearing of a man," one speaker said. "And he married a young girl. From Tiree she was, I am thinking. And such a spinner she was, the thread never broke, and whenever he was coming home the house was neat as a pin and all. But he never could find her at her work whenever he was coming home. And then the lass had a *bairn*, but the child was puny and weak and would not drink milk, but was wailing all the time. Then one night the man dreamed, and his wife was in his dream speaking to him, and she was telling him that the *sithichean* had made away with her and the *bairn*, and that to be getting them back he must be putting them both to the fire, and then the *sithich-*

ean would be letting them go."

"And so, what happened?"

"The man tried with the herbs and such things, but the babe still pined. And it would not thrive on the mother's milk, for it was faerie milk and could not sustain even a changeling. They kept at her for days and days, but the lass would not admit she was of the *sithichean*. Until finally the man had no help for it. He put both her and the babe to the fire."

"*Dia—*"

"And just as he was laying the babe on the fire, there was a huge whirl of wind outside, and there was the host of the *sithichean* riding past his house. The man ran outside and there was his wife herself, seated on a silver horse. Dressed in fine silks, she was, being carried away by a faerie lord, and she was calling out to him. He grabbed for the bridle, and held onto it and grabbed at his wife, and didn't she change her shape into all manner of things—an adder, a ferret, a red fox—and finally he threw the false wife on the fire as well. Although her cries were piteous to hear, he knew it was just the faerie wife that was wailing—" The speaker took another swallow of *uisgebeatha*. "And then there was a clap of lightning all around the house, and the host of *sithichean* disappeared into the sky along with the changelings, and were their cries not horrid to hear, for they had been cheated out of the woman and her child. The man found his wife and son outside where the faeries had dropped them, and the babe was hale and hearty and grew well."

"And what of the man and his wife?"

"The *sithichean* had their revenge on him, for his cattle sickened and died. And he himself drowned some time later."

"And the wife?"

"She died as well. But the child grew up. He was a great hand with horses, that boy. And a good smith, so you know he could not have been of the *sithichean,* since he worked with the iron. But this was long ago. When my auntie was a young girl it happened. I heard of it from her."

"And wasn't there another changeling over in Kintyre? But that one they were not getting back from the *sithichean*. It was not speaking or walking, although it had five years, so it must have been a changeling indeed."

"Aye, if the *sithichean* had the human child for so long as that, they'd no be wanting to part with it."

I shivered at all this talk and drained my cup, thankful that no one had mentioned the bones of the infant we had found in the cave. The talk seemed not to affect Liam however, and soon enough the topic changed to hunting. It seemed that Liam was something of a hunter, or claimed to be at least, and was not shy to be speaking of it either. He started to tell of yet another stag he had pursued over half of Mull, and I grew less and less interested. But we stayed a bit longer, until finally I reminded him they would be feasting up at the dun and he agreed to leave. We made our way back towards Dun Evin, Liam's horse following obediently behind us as we stumbled up the hill. Somehow we managed not to fall down the steep path in the process, for the moon was not yet up and we were somewhat the worse for drink.

We entered the dun, where we found the evening meal well underway. Mariota evidently was spending the night at Aorig's, for I did not see her at the table. I found I had little appetite, and excused myself early to sleep uneasily, dreaming of shining hordes of *sithichean* who lapsed like quicksilver through my hands as I tried to grab and hold them.

CHAPTER 10

I awoke the next morning with a new sense of resolve.

Everything seemed to center around the north of the island, around Balnahard and Carnan Eoin. And so, the skies clearing, I set out towards the area again.

I had asked Mariota to join me, but she did not. "I have not been feeling well, Muirteach," she said. "I am thinking I will just stay here at the dun today and help your aunt with the preparations for the Samhain, or perhaps I will be visiting with Aorig again. I am not feeling like riding up to the end of the island." And so I went without her, taking only Somerled, who loped alongside my borrowed horse.

We made good enough time to the north of the island, although the sky was leaden and the wind blew cold, pushing us onward. I wrapped my *brat* tightly around me, but still I felt the damp creep through the wool like the unseen visitors from the other world that silently entered our dwellings at Samhain. I passed the Tràigh Bàn, not so golden today under the gray clouds, then started the climb between the summits of the two hills towards the tumbled stones that were the remnants of the cairn there. There were some massive stones around the outside of the mass of earth, which was dwarfed by the greater height of Carnan Eoin to my right and the Beinn Beag farther up the track on the left.

The rock on the cairn glistened damply after the rain. I dismounted and walked around the stones until I reached the far side of the rocks. I saw no faerie gold nor marks that anyone had found anything there, but then thought to inspect the top of the mound.

On the top of the mound was a large broken stone and not much else. Somerled, who had clambered up shortly after we arrived, intently nosed around it, digging at the earth with his paws. I whistled for him, thinking some rabbit had made a burrow in the faerie mound, but the stubborn dog ignored me.

I felt my heart beat faster with nerves, or perhaps it was fear. For all that I thought the *sithichean* had not taken Niall, I was not sure about traipsing over the top of the mound where they might dwell. And perhaps I had a presentiment of what I would find.

I took a deep breath, trying to calm the pounding of my heart, and walked towards my dog. He came up to me, tail wagging with pride, holding a small arm, much decayed and gnawed at one end, in his mouth.

I got my dog to loose the arm, then followed him back to the stone. I pushed the rock aside a bit with effort, for it was large and heavy. I saw a shoulder, a bit of blond hair, and more of the body, stained with dirt and somewhat crushed. It looked very little like the boy I remembered, but Somerled had found Niall.

My stomach turned and I shuddered, then retched twice. The sun, barely visible in the gray sky, was already lowering in the west. I watched it for a moment to avoid looking at the corpse. Although I now knew what had become of Niall, I could not face what I had found.

Gillean lived not so far away. I carefully placed the arm with the rest of the body, and then I left that dreadful place. I rode my horse down the track towards his cottage, hoping for a torch and some human companionship to help me deal with the horror I had seen, but I did not find Gillean at home. I had forgotten that tonight was Samhain, when the spirits of the dead visited the living.

I rode over to the huts near the Tràigh Bàn, where Àine lived. A bonfire blazed brightly there, livening the oncoming gray twilight while people gathered around it, talking and joking. They were telling fortunes with hazelnuts, but I think no one had divined that a corpse would be found that grisly evening. Everyone crossed themselves when I told them my news, and the crowd broke into excited talk. A messenger was sent to Dun Evin while some of the men followed me back up the hillside to the cairn with torches as the sun was setting.

We moved the heavy stone atop the cairn completely aside, and found the body, or what remained of it, buried underneath. The skin, greenish and an unnatural red, sloughed loosely off the flesh, and the stench was fierce. Mold grew on the body, and we had to move the remains with great care. It had been some four weeks since the lad went missing. Now we had found Niall, but not his murderer.

We had most of the body disinterred and wrapped in a plaid before my uncle and the Benbecula MacDonald arrived. By this time it had grown dark, although after a time a full Samhain moon rose and cast a pale light on the proceedings. Then we took the poor bundle back to the dun, in a procession lit by the moon and the light of torches.

Sìne, Niall's own mother, set up a wild keening, joined by my aunt Euluasaid. Dòmhnall took one look at the body and rushed out of the hall. Mariota sat white-faced, weeping silently, for all that she had not known the lad. Truly, it was as if the doors between this world and the other world were flung open that dark and deadly Samhain night, what with a corpse of a child lying in the dun and no human yet found to punish for the deed.

After a time the women took the pathetic pile of flesh and

bones to prepare it for burial and the wake that would precede it. I sat with my uncle and the MacDonald, drinking some *uisge-beatha*. It burned my throat but did little to numb the sense of failure I felt. Someone had murdered the boy, and I had yet to find the killer. Of a sudden a louder keening was heard from my aunt's chamber, and one of Euluasaid's maids came running in.

"Muirteach, it is asking for you they are. And the chief himself. You must come at once."

We followed her to the door of my aunt's chamber. The sounds of a woman sobbing and my aunt's murmured words of comfort met us in the hallway. Mariota, white-faced, stood at the door and stopped the MacDonald from pushing his way into the room behind us.

"Just wait a wee while, until he is ready to be seen. Please. Here, can you comfort your wife?" she added as Euluasaid led the woman out of the room.

"Muirteach," Mariota said once they were away, "you must look at this."

The boy's body lay facedown on the table where the women had been preparing the poor corpse for burial. Mariota held the candle close, and its flame illuminated the remains. On the boy's back, despite the decomposition, we could see an ugly wound.

"An arrow wound, it looks like," I observed.

"Indeed," said Mariota. "And this is what was the cause of it."

She walked over to the table, picked up a small wooden plate sitting there, then brought it back to show me. On the plate rested a bloody arrow, roughly worked of flint.

"*Dia*, it is a faerie arrow!" The candle flickering in the room seemed to waver as I spoke.

"Perhaps it is, Muirteach, but I have never seen the like of it before. This is not as finely worked as some are. And usually when folk are taken by the faerie they are not shot like this. They find the faerie arrow nearby after a person is stricken down."

"Aye," I agreed. For it was often enough I had found faerie arrows as a child there on the *machair*. And never had one made a wound like this. "This is an arrow wound, and I think it was a man that shot him."

Gillespic, when he saw the arrow, grew grim. "Indeed it is a faerie arrow, Muirteach, but I am thinking that this is best kept among ourselves. If folk are thinking the *sithichean* are shooting us on their wild hunts, there will be no end of panic. They are already blaming the good folk for every sick *bairn* on the island. I also am thinking it was a man who drew the bow. But what man hunts with faerie arrows?"

I did not know the answer to his question.

Later that long night, Euluasaid asked Malcolm for Dòmhnall, but he was not to be found anywhere. And so, exhausted, we set out to search for him as the dawn slowly grew over the island.

I thought I knew where to look, and again riding north towards Carnan Eoin, I eventually found Dòmhnall sitting in the ruined hut on the Beinn Beag. He sat with his knees drawn up, huddled into a ball, staring over the ruined walls and out over the hills. A wet rain drizzled down, and his plaid was soaked through.

I approached slowly, but he heard my step and turned to look at me, then burst into sobs.

"Muirteach," he cried, "Why were they not taking me? Why did they have to take Niall? I killed him by leaving him here—"

I sat down next to the boy on the wet ground but said nothing. I thought of my young orphaned half sister and half brothers, and felt I had spent far too much time lately trying to comfort children over deaths that were not their fault. In that case also I had not known what to say to them. And now I floundered, trying to find some words of comfort for my nephew.

"No, no, indeed you did not kill him," I finally said when his sobbing had diminished somewhat. "You must not be thinking in such a way. You did not shoot the arrow, Dòmhnall. You did not kill him."

"But I should not have left him there. It has all been my fault."

Nothing I could say could convince him otherwise. Dòmhnall in his grief and his guilt was as stubborn as his foster-brother had been in his search for the faerie. And I myself felt my own failure, and could find few words to convince the lad he was not at fault. Finally I gave up trying, and attempted to interest him in some food.

"Here is a bannock and some speckled bread from the meal last night. Come, eat. It will not bring Niall back to starve yourself to death."

At the smell of the fresh baked bread, Somerled pushed his way over to us and sat looking hopeful, his eyes glued to the bread in my hand and the hairs on his gray muzzle quivering in anticipation.

"For if you are not wanting it, Dòmhnall, I am thinking that Somerled here will be willing to eat it for you."

At this the boy brightened a little. He asked for some bannock, which I was happy to give him, but then he offered it to the dog and did not eat it himself. Then, after the dog finished wolfing down the bread, the boy hugged the dog tightly and buried his head in Somerled's wiry fur. I could see from the shake of his shoulders that the lad was grieving again.

I patted his shoulder and the shaking eased a little, but I could still hear the muffled sound of sobbing.

"Now, Dòmhnall, come." I tried to sound authoritative. "Your mother is aye sick to think of you being lost, and your father has that glint in his eye." I did not add that Gillespic looked sick with worry as well at the thought of his missing son. "We'd best be getting back to the dun and seeing them. It will not do to worry them so, not now."

Dòmhnall raised his face from Somerled's flank. "Aye, Muirteach," he finally agreed. He swallowed and wiped at the tearstains on his cheeks. "I will come with you."

And that, at least, was a great relief to me on such a bitter day.

All Souls' Day was foggy, and my vision came to pass. The keening of the women filled my ears as I followed the sad procession down the beach to the boat that bore young Niall and his grieving parents back to his island home. I stayed on Colonsay, not wanting to return to Islay. I had found Niall, but not his murderer. I expected to hear from the Lord of the Isles regarding the matter—but no messengers or news came from Islay, although His Lordship's men returned to Finlaggan. Perhaps the Shepherd of the Isles was too concerned with politics to be worrying over the death of a child on Colonsay, even his own grandson.

With the MacDonalds gone back to Benbecula, things on the island and at my uncle's dun quieted a bit. Aunt Euluasaid began to put her household back to rights after the upset His Lordship's men had caused. The MacRuaris stayed on, seeming to be in no great haste to be leaving the island, and I puzzled over which woman Raghnall was courting.

Liam MacLean also remained. I wondered querulously if he had any duties at all on Mull, such a man of leisure he seemed to be. He appeared in little hurry to return to his home there.

But this wondering still left me on Colonsay with the mystery of who killed a young boy to solve.

The morning after this dawned fair, and Liam was all for hunting again. Apparently he felt that our sojourn to Donald Dubh's had made us comrades, for he asked me to join him. I did, borrowing a mount from my uncle and bringing Somerled with us.

"And how were you coming to own a deerhound?" inquired Liam, a bit jealously I thought, with some satisfaction.

"My uncle was giving him to me." I did not add that Somerled was a pathetic hunter. If we were lucky enough to find game today, Liam would discover that for himself.

I was thinking we should try the south of the island, but Liam was all for heading to the north again. I wondered at that, but did not gainsay him, as I myself had my own interest in that end of the island. We turned our horses in that direction, but saw little enough game—or islanders, for that matter. The horses were eager for exercise, and soon enough we found ourselves at the far end of the island, a bit beyond the nunnery. There was a fine bit of open ground that led down to another sandy beach under the shadow of a large outcropping of rocks.

We stopped to rest the horses and to eat some of the oatcakes and cheese we had brought with us. Somerled, after begging for some scraps, lay down and looked as though he would sleep. It did not sound like too bad a thought to me, for I had something of a headache, brought on by the drink last night and my unsettled sleep.

"I'm thinking Somerled and I will wait here a wee while while you go on a bit," I said, tethering my horse and arranging my cloak for a bit of a pillow in a hollow between two low hills. The early afternoon sun was warm enough, and I had no wish to see what was up on the north coast of the island. I'd been there often enough. Too often lately, I thought dourly. Liam assented with alacrity. I thought he was glad to be rid of me, and he set out over the rocks towards the standing stones past Cnoc Cnorr. I laid my head on my cloak and closed my eyes for a bit, the warm and lazy bulk of Somerled serving as a windbreak.

I had not intended to sleep, but I did. I woke hearing voices, a man's and a woman's, carried to me on the breeze, but I could not catch their words. Then I thought I heard the sound of crying, then quiet, just the wind. I sat up, stretched and stood up to look, but could not see above the hollow. Curious, I climbed to the top of the hill, followed by Somerled, but no one was there, just an eagle circling overhead. Perhaps the noise of the mysterious speakers, whoever they had been, had disturbed the great bird.

I walked back down, mounted my horse and set off towards Cnoc Cnorr with the thought in my mind of finding Liam. I had not gone far when I saw a lone rider—Liam. He had had no luck hunting, he said, and had seen no game. Just the same eagle who still circled in the sky.

I wondered at the voices I had heard, and it was on the tip of my tongue to ask him of them. But as Liam denied seeing anyone else while he had been hunting, I did not ask him more of it.

We started back towards Dun Evin, passing no one for some time, although closer to Balnahard one of the sisters walked, carrying a basket of something and headed towards the nunnery.

On the way back to Dun Evin, Liam began to talk of the hunting on Jura and how fine it was. I let him ramble on, still puzzling over the voices I thought I had heard. Perhaps they had only been a dream, some fancy. As we reached the point where the path branches off towards Bride's well, Liam turned his horse in that direction.

"And where are you off to?" I questioned, sounding like a

shrewish wife. But the dark was growing, and it did not seem to me to be the time to be off riding.

"I am just wanting a short ride to be clearing my head," returned Liam. "It will be bright enough for an hour or so yet."

So I left him there and made my way up to the dun, while Liam rode his horse up along the trail.

That night I enjoyed the feasting at my uncle's dun, but Liam did not return.

"Och, perhaps he got lost and slept out in the open," said my uncle, little concerned when Euluasaid pointed this out to him. "Or took shelter someplace. He's a grown man and can find his way back here again right enough."

CHAPTER 11

That night in the hall Fergus began to talk about our trip to the witch-woman on Jura, and Mariota listened avidly.

"I have heard of old Gormal," she said. "People on Islay visit her from time to time. I have heard she is a good healer, with a fine remedy for the falling sickness, and other things as well."

"But you were never seeing her over there?" I asked, curious. I had thought that Mariota and her father knew every healer in the Hebrides.

"I was never going, but I am thinking my father did visit her once or twice. But I can not be remembering what he was telling me of her—just, I think, that she kept the old ways. There is certainly nothing of the black witchcraft about her. Perhaps she is a white witch. And I think he was saying that she knew some good remedies, but he could not be getting her to share them with him." Mariota's brow furrowed as she thought. "Aye, that was it. He was saying she was the guardian of a well and a suicide's skull. And that the water of the well, if it is drunk from that skull, can cure the falling sickness."

She paused, then said a minute later, with a brighter look to her eyes, "Muirteach, perhaps we should be going to visit her again. I am curious about her and her medicines."

It felt good to see Mariota interested in something and not speaking of shutting herself up in a nunnery, so I agreed readily. And I had my own reasons for wanting to visit the woman again.

"Aye. And although her scrying was not successful before,

perhaps now that we know poor Niall is dead, she might scry again and see the killer. For I am not thinking the *sithichean* killed him, but with all the clues I've been finding, they might as well have."

So we made our plans to visit Jura again. Why my uncle was willing to lend me a boat I could not understand, but he seemed perfectly happy with the arrangement, only warning me "not to sink this one." Seamus wanted to go and so did Aorig, and so the four of us set out in a small boat of my uncle's for the trip to Jura the next morning with fair, although cold, weather.

The brisk wind pushed our boat across the strait, and we approached the same cove we had visited before. There was another boat beached there, with a distinctive carved prow on it, and I wondered if some other folk were visiting the witch. For I myself, unlike Mariota, felt that there was something uncanny about old Gormal, and I was glad I did not have the falling sickness. The thought of drinking from the skull of a suicide did not appeal.

As we climbed up the narrow track, I saw some rowan growing by the sides of the walk. Surely a black witch would not have rowan growing so close to her home, I thought. Although Mariota had suggested the trip and was enthusiastic about it, I myself found I had some worries about possibly putting her into harm's way yet another time. If indeed Gormal was a witch.

We neared the door and knocked, but no one answered. So we found ourselves some fine large rocks to sit on and waited for her return.

It was not Gormal, but a man who came around another path leading down to the cave from the top of the hill. He had a deer slung over his shoulder, carrying it easily despite its weight, and looked to be just returning from the hunt. He stared at us a moment but said nothing, just let the deer down onto the earth as he stood in front of the witch's doorway. His eyes flicked at us and then he looked at the ground, glancing sidewise at us from time to time.

"We are wishing to see Gormal," Aorig finally spoke when the man did not. "Can you understand me?"

The man nodded but did not speak.

"Are you knowing when she will be returning?" asked Mariota.

The man nodded a second time, and motioned for us to enter the cave. Then he left us, still without having spoken a word. Outside we could hear noise as he strung the deer up and started to skin it.

We stood uncomfortably for a few moments, then finally sat on the wooden stools and waited.

"Perhaps he will be her servant. He is an odd one, that man," said Aorig, a little nervously I thought.

"Yes. He must be mute," commented Mariota.

While we waited I looked around at the old witch's cave. The chest she had taken the silver bowl from on our first visit lay open, and I was curious as to what lay inside it.

Gormal appeared soon after that.

"You are back again," she said to me. "Whatever it is you are searching for, you will not find it here."

Mariota interjected, "Please do not be minding him. It was doing me a favor he was entirely, to bring me to you. I am Fearchar Beaton's daughter—the physician from Islay. You have heard of him?"

Gormal's manner softened a little. "He is a good man. He has visited me here. Twice he came."

"I am his daughter," Mariota continued. "And when I heard Muirteach had seen you before, nothing would do but that he must bring me myself to meet you. For you see I also am a healer, and I have much to learn, being young."

"You could not be learning from your father then?" asked Gormal.

"I have learned much from him. But I was hearing you had a remedy for the falling sickness, and other remedies—"

"Indeed. I have many remedies for many things. But I may not be sharing them with every woman who fancies she is a healer, even if she is one of the famous Beatons."

Mariota said nothing to that, but I could tell from the way she bit upon her lip that the woman's words had stung her.

It was Aorig who broke the silence.

"Were you hearing of the young boy missing on Colonsay?"

"Indeed. For that one," and she gestured to me, "was here, with the boy's mother."

Aorig nodded. "That was the way of it. But were you hearing the last?"

"It's little enough news I hear here, quiet as it is. And little enough news I care to hear. I just wish to live here undisturbed. By the likes of you."

"But the lad was found dead," Seamus blurted out. "Under a cairn. It is said the *sithichean* killed him."

"Well, I am knowing nothing of that. And nothing of the *sithichean*, either. As he knows full well." Gormal motioned again towards me. "The scrying did not work that day, and I will not try again in that matter. And if none of you are needing any remedies, it's little enough I have to say to you, except that the winds will soon be changing, and if you are not leaving soon it's a hard time you will have getting back to Colonsay."

At this a draft whistled through the cave, and I felt a sudden chill. I wondered if she was putting the evil eye upon us or on our boat, or summoning up a storm to confound us. I stood up to leave, for I was not liking this.

"Come, let us be going." I gave her a coin. "We are sorry to have bothered you, and I am not liking to trouble you for nothing. Thank you for your ale."

Gormal took the coin and nodded at this, and the others stood. We left and returned to our boat.

"I am sorry, *mo chridhe*, that you were learning nothing of her cures," I said to Mariota as we embarked.

"She was not forthcoming, was she? Perhaps she is right. I am but a young *amadain*, and will never make a true healer." Mariota appeared to be close to tears. Keeping her eyes carefully fixed on the horizon, she wrapped her blue mantle tightly against her as the sea wind blew and we entered the strait between Colonsay and Jura. "You have a fine touch with the healing," I said, trying to comfort her. "Do not be taking her words to heart. She is just a bitter old woman who lives alone in the caves there." I did not add that I prayed the bitter old woman had not set the evil eye on us for disturbing her as we did.

It seemed she had not, for we had a fine enough trip back to Colonsay but arrived well after dark. There were torches flaring and a group of people milled around the landing site at Scalasaig. I wondered what had happened—this time of year most people were snug inside by their hearths in the dark evenings.

I found out soon enough for as we beached the boat, a friend of Seamus's came running towards us.

"You are back at last," he cried.

"Whatever is it then?"

The lad paused, then excitedly announced his news. "It is that Liam MacLean, the one from Mull. The one who was drinking with you that night at Donald Dubh's. And riding that great big gray horse around here and there, all over the island."

"Yes, what of him?" I asked, interrupting.

"He was found up by Balnahard, knocked from his horse, senseless."

CHAPTER 12

"Is he dead?" I asked.

The lad shook his head. "No, no, but he is sore injured and may die soon enough. He is up at the dun with your auntie and the MacPhee."

And so it was quickly enough that we made our way there after leaving Aorig and Seamus in the village.

Euluasaid met us in the hall.

"Indeed, and you were already hearing of it then? A sin and a sad thing it is, and himself so witty and handsome and always such a friend to Niall and Dòmhnall." Euluasaid's voice came near to breaking as she spoke Niall's name, but after a moment she steadied herself and continued. "And a shame on our island, it is, that such things are happening here. In truth, I think the world has gone mad this year."

Liam lay senseless on my aunt's second-best bedstead, his breathing even, but with no recognition or awareness in his eyes. He seemed to be in a deep sleep. Mariota examined him while the rest of us looked on. But she seemed hesitant when she finally spoke.

"I am wishing I knew more—I am wishing my father was here. I have only seen one case of something like this. A man slipped out on the cliffs as he looked for bird's eggs, and got a fearsome blow to the head. He never woke. But he did not die. It was as though his soul was caught between the living and the dead."

"What finally happened?" I asked.

"His wife nursed him, but he never woke or spoke, not for years. Although he would open his eyes and swallow the gruel she spooned into his mouth, he never knew her. The poor woman thought the faerie had stolen him, but then one day, after some five years had passed, he did wake and recognize her. But he did not know his child, for his child had grown older. And the man could not walk well, his joints had stiffened so."

"But he did wake."

"Aye. But he died thereafter, of the lung fever. It was sad. And my father did not know how to wake him, and I do not know what to be doing for Liam now." Mariota saw to the poultices and looked at the blow to his head. "How was he injured?"

"That Eachann Beag found him," replied my uncle. "The old man was out looking for his wandering goat."

"That would be Muireal," I added, remembering the old man.

"Well, I am not knowing the name of the goat. But Eachann Beag found him lying in a ravine."

Liam did not look so handsome as he lay there senseless, but it was easy enough to see the large bloodied wound to the back of his skull.

"And they were thinking he fell from his horse?" I asked Gillespic.

My uncle nodded. "Well, the horse was found nearby grazing as happy as you please. And there are no other wounds. So what were they to think?"

Mariota shook her head. "I do not think this wound was made from a fall. I think someone struck him hard from behind. See here on his trews, the mud on the knees? Perhaps he was kneeling down."

"Perhaps," I said. "But there is mud enough on this island to get some on your trews easy enough."

"Well, that is what I am thinking," said Mariota, sounding a little hurt. "But I am young and not knowing all of it, and perhaps I am wrong. That old hag on Jura would not trust my judgment. So why should you be trusting what I say?"

I looked at her and thought I saw her lip quivering, although I was surprised she would take affront at my words.

"I was just saying, Mariota, that he might not have been kneeling. Perhaps he did fall from his horse."

"Indeed," replied Mariota, "you must have the right of it, Muirteach," the quaver in her voice replaced by a harder note.

"So you were visiting the witch, were you?" asked Gillespic. "And how was that?"

"She was not overly gracious," I replied, and that matter was dropped.

"But who would be wanting to hurt that MacLean?" mused my uncle. "He does not know that many people here."

"Although who knows where he went when he was off riding? He said he was hunting, but it's little enough the game he brought back to the dun. For such a talker as he was, with all the stories of his deer on Mull, you would expect him to be having more success with the hunt here."

"Perhaps he was frightening them away with his chattering."

"He was a talkative one. Perhaps he met someone on the island, and they grew angry over something. Then they fought and the other person struck him."

I found I could easily imagine that, as I had not enjoyed Liam's stories overmuch myself. But I felt guilty for such thoughts with him lying there senseless and pale. Although he continued to breathe shallowly, he did not rouse to our voices. And there were no scratches or other bruises on Liam's body that would indicate a fight had gone on, although in the candlelight it was difficult to tell for certain.

"What of the MacRuaris?" I asked. "Where were they?"

"They were away back to Benbecula just this morning, early. They had been planning to leave for some days, but the weather had not been good for sailing. But it cleared this morning as you know, for you yourselves went to Jura."

"But Liam would have been injured the day before that. So they could have done it and left before he was found."

"Well," Gillespic said grudgingly, for he liked the MacRuaris, "I can be sending some men after them to see if they know anything of the matter. But what reason would they have to be attacking Liam MacLean?"

I had no answer for that question.

The morning light did not reveal anything new, and Liam's condition did not improve. After a time I set out for the north of the island.

I stopped by Eachann Beag's home. The old man was glad enough to take a break from the work he was doing in the byre and invited me to sit down and have a dram with him. Soon enough the talk turned to Liam, and nothing would do but that the old man would tell me every detail of what he had been doing when he found him.

"It was that Muireal again that I was looking for. She is a wanderer, that one. But it was a lucky chance I came upon him that day. A pity it was he fell from his horse in such a way."

"So you are thinking he fell then?" I asked.

"Indeed yes. We've no murderers here," Eachann insisted stubbornly. "The *sithichean* were taking that young boy that was found in their hill and the other one, too, from that village. And this one fell from his horse."

How he could believe that I did not know, but I let it pass.

"And were you seeing faerie lights that night? Or have you

seen any more strangers?"

Whatever or whoever had injured Liam, I did not think it was the *sithichean*. Nor did I think for one minute that Liam had fallen from his horse. But whoever attacked him might have carried a torch.

Eachann shook his head no. "But the rain was such that I was not going outside. I brought the animals in—all except that Muireal, that goat I was not finding until the next day—and I sat by the fire that night. I told her, just, that she would have to be out in the rain all the long night as she was wandering so."

I thanked him for the drink, took my leave, and continued back towards Carnan Eoin, where Liam's body had been found. I had not liked the man overmuch; in truth I had envied him his looks and his strength, but today he lay unconscious, almost like the dead, and I was hale and hearty. I told myself I would make amends for my earlier envy by finding his attacker. For I did not for one instant believe he had fallen from his horse.

I rode leisurely in the direction of Carnan Eoin, and when I got to the gully where Liam had been found I dismounted. I found a rock, traces of blood still remaining in the clefts of it. Eachann had told me Liam had been lying facedown and, from the look of him, Mariota had thought that someone had hit him at the base of the skull with the stone. Here was the rock itself to prove her right. Nearby I saw some depressions in the ground, perhaps the marks of someone kneeling on the wet ground. But who had struck him, and why? Why had Liam dismounted? What had he seen? Somehow I did not think it was the red deer he had been tracking that day, but a much more dangerous and elusive quarry, one that had cost him his life's blood.

I thought of Liam and his boastful manner of speaking. If he had kept quieter, I mused, he might still be uninjured. For I was beginning to have an idea as to why he had been attacked if not who had done it. It was an ugly idea, indeed.

When I arrived back at the dun, I sought out Mariota. I felt I had offended her the night before and wanted to tell her of the rock I had seen. I found Mariota, along with Euluasaid, gathering some herbs together in my aunt's storeroom."

"Muirteach, you must be accompanying me back up to the nunnery at Cill Chaitrìona," she told me abruptly before I had the chance to tell her my news. She would not meet my eyes.

"And why is that?" I asked, my heart sinking like a stone falling into deep loch waters.

"I am going back to the sisters, for another retreat."

Euluasaid looked apologetically at me.

"Muirteach, she is wanting to go . . ." Her voice trailed off as she saw the look in my eyes. "I will leave Muirteach here to help you with the herbs," she continued after a pause in a brisk tone. And with that my aunt left us alone.

"Mo chridhe," I said. "Why must you do this?"

Mariota did not meet my eyes.

"It is just," she finally said, "I feel safe there. Oh, Muirteach, can you not understand? But why should you? Even I do not understand myself at all since last June. I dream of the church and the rope around my neck. And all that water—. I can not stand to be alone, and yet I can not stand the noise of large gatherings. I startle for no reason. My heart pounds like a wild thing, and I can not stop it. All I can do is listen to it hammering in my chest. And now that woman Gormal is saying I will never be a healer, and it is believing her I am, for I can not even heal myself."

"And what is your father saying of all of this?" I asked. "For he is a fine healer, and mayhap he can help you."

"I can not tell him, Muirteach. He was so grateful to have me back unharmed by that madman. How can I tell him of it at all, at all? I could not be worrying him so."

My heart sank again at her words. For wasn't it my own foolishness that had put her in such danger last summer, when we had followed that madman through the whirlpool and over to Islay?

"But what of Liam? Surely my aunt will be needing you to help nurse him?"

Mariota was adamant. "She can nurse him as well herself. I am no healer. That old witch spoke truly."

I sat down on a bench and gestured for her to sit next to me. To my surprise, she did.

"*Mo chridhe*, it is sorry I am to hear about all this. I failed you there on Mull."

Mariota started to cry.

"No, Muirteach, you did not. You saved me on the Oa. He would have taken me over the cliffs with him."

Haltingly I reached out and put my arm around her while she sobbed. I had never held her so close before. I breathed in the elderflower scent she used, feeling her trembling next to me with her crying, and I felt like weeping myself for the ruins of all that might have been between us, and now would not be.

"And so you are going to Cill Chaitríona?"

"Aye, for I do not know what else to do."

I turned to face her. Her lovely face was just inches from me. Awkwardly, I put my hand up to caress her hair. In the dim light of the storeroom, I fancied it shone like the sun shining through the clouds after a wet day. After a moment she pulled away from me a bit. We remained sitting side by side on the bench.

I took hold of her hand and held it, massaging her palm with my fingers. Mariota did not pull away from my touch.

"But what of your father? Surely you can not be running off to a nunnery without his permission."

Mariota bristled at this. I could feel it in the sudden tension in her hand, but I did not let go.

"I am of age. I can do as I wish."

"But will it not worry him?"

"I hope not."

I felt her relax a little as I continued to hold her hand.

"I—I will write him and tell him of my plans and of my reasons for going." Mariota looked at me, and started to smile. "Muirteach, I am only going a few miles away. I am not becoming an anchoress! Surely they will let me see my father and explain myself. Certainly before I take my final vows."

Cill Chaitrìona might have been only a few miles away on this very same small island of Colonsay, yet I felt Mariota might have been going instead to far-off Constantinople. But how could I gainsay her? I had no right. And especially not as it was my own poor judgment last summer that had wounded her so.

"Well then, go if you must." But my heart was not in the words, and I bent my head towards hers and tenderly kissed her on the lips.

She put her arms around me and drew me closer to her. We kissed gently for a moment, and although I had dreamed of kissing her before, this kiss had more of a farewell in it than the happiness I had dreamed of.

After a moment we drew apart.

"I am sorry, dear heart," I finally said, awkward again. "But if you are to be a nun, I could not let you go without at least one kiss."

Mariota nodded and wiped at her eyes with the back of her hand.

"Indeed, Muirteach. I am glad you did not let me go without a kiss."

For a moment I had the mad thought of kissing her again, and not so gently this time. But I hesitated, for if she was truly wanting to take holy vows what would be the point? The moment passed. Mariota stood and straightened her back with resolution.

"Well, I should just be getting these herbs together. I am not wanting to go empty-handed up there, and I am thinking the sisters will be able to use these. I have some tincture of poppy I can bring them. That is costly, and hard to come by."

I nodded.

"Such a strange dowry!" she added, laughing a little bit. But I fancied her voice had no real mirth in it.

"Well, what would you expect from one of the famous Beatons?" I said, also trying to joke about it. "I will take you when you are ready to go to Balnahard."

Mariota nodded tightly. "Good. I am thinking it will not be until tomorrow."

"Tomorrow, then."

I left her and went down into Scalasaig with Somerled to Donald Dubh's, and got myself very drunk on *uisgebeatha*. Then I staggered the short distance to my house in the village and collapsed in a stupor on an old pile of rank bracken. I did not return to the dun but slept at my own house in the village that night. But my sleep was troubled by unpleasant dreams.

It was mid-morning the next day that Mariota and I set out for Balnahard. I brought Somerled along, for I surmised I would be glad of the dog's company after I had left Mariota with the nuns. I felt awkward after our kiss in the storeroom the day before, and perhaps Mariota did as well for we did not speak of it. In fact, we spoke little at all. Somerled chased rabbits ineffectually and lagged behind our horses much of the way, leaving the two of us riding quietly towards the north end of the island. I felt I was riding to my own funeral.

Despite our silence the miles passed, and soon enough it was we had reached the nunnery. The abbess was surprised to see

Mariota, but admitted her willingly. Once again I was left outside the gates, alone except for my dog.

Some clouds rolled in and it began to rain in earnest. I cursed the weather and then cursed Mariota and then, feeling no better than before, I began the ride back to Dun Evin, leading the horse Mariota had been riding behind me. It threw a shoe, and I was forced to stop near old Àine's cottage, near the Tràigh Bàn, and look for a smith. I did not find one, at least not one who was able to work—Mochta was ill, his wife told me, and the coals in his smithy were out and cold. By now the rain was coming in sheets, almost sideways, blowing in on the Tràigh Bàn from the water and the direction of the Sound of Mull and the mainland. Somerled and I took shelter under a tree, although we might as well have been in the wide open for all the shelter it provided. My dog began to whine as rain dripped off our noses.

I stood forlornly on the cliff overlooking the Tràigh Bàn, but then I remembered old Àine. Surely she would not begrudge me some shelter on a day like this.

I made my way towards her cottage. She heard the noise of my horses and the whining of my dog and came to the door. At first she did not seem to remember me and looked at me in a puzzled way until I mentioned Fergus, and then she nodded with more recognition and bade me come in out of the wet. Although my mood was sour and my head somewhat aching from my overindulgence of the night before, my mood improved once I was under a dry roof. Somerled also seemed content and lay down at my feet, a wet bundle of smelly dog. Àine gave me some fresh oatcakes and for all that her memory was failing, her baking abilities had not failed her in the least. I shared a cake with my dog and after wolfing it down, he promptly fell asleep at my feet by the hearth.

Despite the pangs of hunger in my stomach and the sadness

in my heart, I found I also did feel better out of the wet. As the rain drummed on the thatch, I listened drowsily to the old woman's stories—the least I could do, I mused, in return for her hospitality. But I paid scant attention until she mentioned the *sithichean* again.

"And so have you been seeing their lights again?" I asked her.

"And who was telling you that I had been seeing their lights?" demanded the old woman, apparently forgetting the stories she had told us a few weeks earlier.

"Why, you yourself were, Granny. You were saying you had seen lights on the hills above the Tràigh Bàn."

She looked at me blankly. "I am not remembering that. It is that woman from near the Beinn Beag. She is the one that deals with the *sithichean.*"

"What woman would that be, Granny?"

"The one that lives there in that hut, near the Beinn Beag it is."

Now I was totally confused, for I had combed over that area time and time again, searching for Niall. There was no hut there, although there were a few ruins. But perhaps Àine had lost her sense of the years and was speaking of someplace long gone. And I was a guest in her home, so I humored her.

"And what does she have to do with the *sithichean?*" I asked.

"Was I not telling you of it that time you came with Fergus? She must have dealings with them, for they took her child and left a changeling in its place."

"And how were you knowing this?"

"It was easy enough to see. The child did not speak, but grew large and strong and ate everything she gave it. But he was never speaking."

"And where are they the now?"

Àine looked confused. "Are they not there now? They were living there, just near the Beinn Beag with her parents. It is a fine steading. Indeed it is."

"What of her son's father?"

Àine shrugged her shoulders. "I am not knowing. Perhaps he himself was of the *sithichean,* and that is why the child is a changeling." She crossed herself. "They can not be bothering me," she continued with some emphasis, "for do I not have that fine rowan tree growing just by the door of the house there outside? And I am never forgetting to leave some milk for them down in the gulley. Good milk with fine cream on it."

"Have you ever seen their treasure?"

She laughed. "Now what would an old woman like me be knowing of their treasure? No, I have never seen it."

I persisted. "But, Granny, I am thinking you must have seen many strange things in your life. Why should you not be knowing of their treasure, since you are knowing so much of the *sithichean?*"

"It was for that I was planting the rowan tree outside, as a young girl just married, when I came here with my Angus. It was to keep them away, it was. Angus was saying we must plant the rowan to keep them from coming back for their own. And they have never bothered us for all these long years. But I should not speak of it. Angus would be angered if he was to know."

"But, Granny, is not your Angus buried in the churchyard these many years?"

Àine looked confused, then laughed in embarrassment. "Aye, so he is indeed. It was a fever he was getting that took him away from me. And what is your name?"

I had told her my name many times before. "I am Muirteach," I repeated with some impatience in my voice. "I am a friend of Fergus's, your nephew."

"Oh, so you are not knowing the other man, then?"

"Who would that be, Granny? When I came your way before, it was Fergus I was with. What other man?"

"Och, I can not remember his name. But he was here, asking about the faerie."

"And what did he look like?"

"He was tall, and with blond hair. And he rode a fine horse."

That sounded like Liam.

"But when was he here, Granny?"

"A long time ago it was."

"And what was he wanting?"

"Oh, the same as you. It was full of questions he was, about the *sithichean* and their gold. But I was not telling him all that I know. For Angus would be angry if I was speaking of it at all, at all. You should see my Angus," she continued. "A fine, braw man he is, with those broad shoulders and that red hair he has. And a fine hunter he is as well. He will be coming back soon," she continued. "And I am thinking he will be bringing a deer with him."

With that, Àine began speaking of her long-dead husband as though she expected him to walk in the door at any minute, and try as I might I could not be getting her to speak more of the *sithichean* or of their treasure. By this time the rain had diminished to a mere drizzle and so, after listening to a few more stories of Angus, I roused my dog. I bade the old woman farewell and made my way back to Dun Evin, leading the lame horse behind me, leaving the old woman standing in her doorway sheltered by her rowan tree.

CHAPTER 13

I arrived back at Dun Evin to find great excitement. A ship had put in from Islay, with a message from His Lordship. He was wanting both my uncle and myself for a council, which was to take place in his hall at Finlaggan. We were to leave at once, and I quickly made my preparations, gathering my writing materials and putting them in my satchel. I had learned to read and write as a child at the priory, and I had often acted as scribe for my uncle even before the events of last summer that had brought me to the notice of His Lordship and left me with the title of "the Keeper of the Records."

I left Somerled with Seamus and Aorig, much to my little half brother Sean's delight. He fancied Somerled as a substitute for a horse of his own and often tried to ride the great lout of a dog.

We left the next morning and crossed to Islay with no difficulty. A small council convened the next day to deal with some matters regarding the MacRuaris and the amount of fighting men and galleys they were expected to supply to His Lordship; Himself was wanting it increased somewhat, while the MacRuaris were saying the original agreement should stand. However, the matter was easily settled and, not surprisingly, in favor of the Lord of the Isles.

The agreement duly decided, I finished the notes in the record book, made a copy for the MacRuaris, and sealed the book in its richly carved wooden chest. Then I left it with His

Lordship's librarian.

The two MacRuaris who had been on Colonsay had accompanied their chief to Finlaggan. Gillespic's man had not found them in Benbecula, so I took this chance to question them over some claret in the great hall. From the look of them, the two men had already been at the drink some. There was not a great deal else to do in November, and the weather this day was gray and rainy.

"And so you have not been finding whoever it was that killed the young boy?" asked Griogair. "A great pity that is, indeed and indeed. Not the least of it that the Benbecula MacDonald is still thinking we were killing the lad. He has demanded an honor price from us, and I for one will not be paying it. After all, was it not Raghnall's own son he was shooting so long ago? And we are innocent in this matter. So he will not be getting an honor price from me for this. It was not I who was killing his son."

"Indeed," I agreed, attempting to sound sympathetic. Privately I thought if Griogair had not killed the boy, well, that said nothing as to what Raghnall might have done. "No, we have found nothing of the murderer. Perhaps it was truly the *sithichean,*" I answered, "For he was killed with a faerie arrow."

"Shot with a faerie arrow?" Raghnall crossed himself. "*Dia!* I have never heard of the *sithichean* making wounds that draw blood with their arrows."

"Aye," added Griogair. "Usually you find them beside you, and then you are struck by the arrow. But there is no blood nor any wound that you can see. They must have been aye angry with the lad to shoot him like that. Poor boy, to anger them so."

Raghnall poured himself more claret. "He minded me of my son. I would never have harmed the lad."

"You are not knowing the half of it."

"Indeed?" asked Raghnall, draining his glass of claret and

setting it down on the table. "What is the other half of it, then, Muirteach?"

"It is that Liam MacLean. He was found sore injured, also up near the Carnan Eoin. They are saying he fell from his horse and was hitting his head."

Either the MacRuaris were good actors, or they had known nothing of Liam's misadventure.

"And is he dead then?" asked Raghnall.

"No. He is up at the dun, but he lies there senseless, like a dead man. Yet he still breathes."

"That is a great pity," observed Griogair, his lean face thoughtful. "I pray he recovers well. But he was a wild rider, always taking chances he was."

"He was ready enough with his silver," interjected Raghnall. "It's many the times he was treating us down at that wee alehouse in Scalasaig."

"And where was he getting that money from? He was only a younger son, just running the odd errand for Lachlan Lubanach MacLean. Perhaps the MacLean was just paying him to adorn the hall, with his looks as good as they are. But I am not thinking that the MacLean is all that generous with his silver," mused Griogair. "Well, I am sad to hear the news for all that. And I am thinking there will be many women on Mull who will be sad to hear of it, as well."

"And not on Colonsay? Sure, he was there often enough to have a woman there."

"He was never speaking to me of any women on Colonsay," said Griogair. "Just of the hunt. He was a man for the hunt, he was."

"Aye. Well, let us drink to his health then," said the older man, and we drank a toast to Liam.

Just as we were draining the last of the claret, one of His Lordship's henchmen called me over.

"Himself is wanting to speak with you. He is wanting to know what has been happening over there on that small island." I bristled at this offense to Colonsay but controlled myself. "That MacDonald from Benbecula is all wroth about it, and he is son to His Lordship," explained the man as he walked with me to the solar, as if I did not know that. Inside I found Gillespic and the Lord of the Isles seated at a small table while a brazier warmed the room, taking November chill away from the stone walls.

"And so it is Muirteach," observed His Lordship evenly. "Your uncle was telling me some of what has been happening on Colonsay. So they are saying that young Niall was spirited away by the *sithichean?* Now would you truly be expecting the boy's father or myself, his own grandfather, to be believing that?" His voice was not so even now.

I explained about finding the boy's body with the faerie arrow embedded in its back.

"Yes, well, for all the stories I have heard of the *sithichean,* they are not leaving the corpses behind them," observed the Lord of the Isles dryly. "He was my grandson," he observed, as if we were not already all too cognizant of that fact.

"Indeed, your Lordship, I am thinking the cause of his death is something else entirely." I explained about the gold bangle Gillean had found and the faerie ring Euluasaid had shown me. "I am thinking that someone found gold there, and the boy got in the way of it all and was slain over it. He was a curious lad, and brave," I added, hoping to defuse a little of His Lordship's anger. "He was always investigating here and there. He could have found the gold and been killed by someone for it. But I am not knowing who that person is yet."

"And what of the islanders? Are they in a panic?"

"Indeed no," my uncle assured the MacDonald. "They are saying that Liam fell from his horse. If they are believing that young Niall was killed by the faerie, well, perhaps they are worried about that. Who would not be? But it is common knowledge the lad was headstrong, what with his digging into the *sithean,* and all. So I am thinking most folk believe the good folk were within their rights to be stealing him away and left his corpse there, killed with one of their own arrows, as a warning."

His Lordship looked intently at my uncle. "But that is not what you are believing."

"No. I am agreeing with Muirteach. Someone is on the trail of some gold, and young Niall paid for it with his life. And Liam nearly so."

"What of this Liam? Are you thinking he knew of the gold?"

"We are not sure," I told His Lordship. "But he was free with his money for a landless younger son and an errand boy of Lachlan Lubanach's. Still, he was attacked and nearly killed. He can not be the killer we are seeking."

"Well, find the man, Muirteach," admonished the Lord of the Isles. "And if you are finding some gold as well, well, that is all to the good. I respect the good people, but I would be willing to take a bit of their gold for all the trouble this is causing me. That son of mine will make mischief if he can over this with the MacRuaris. They are not liking each other well, and even without the death of his son, there has been constant trouble. As if those MacRuaris were not enough trouble on their own," added His Lordship. In this I believe the MacDonald referred to his first wife, that Amie MacRuari whom he had put aside some years earlier. She still vexed him at times.

"So find the killer, Muirteach," he repeated, swirling the dregs of the wine in his silver goblet, "and the gold as well. The sooner it is done, the better it will be."

And with that, he dismissed us, turning to some other chieftains who had been ushered into the solar by his retainer.

We exited the solar. I smarted from the abrupt dismissal. My uncle took it in his stride, being more used to dealing with His Lordship over the years, and took himself off to speak with one of the MacInnes he spied lounging on one of the benches in the hall. I looked around and groaned inwardly when I saw a slightly stooped man, slender, with a kind face and yellow hair now going to gray. Fearchar Beaton. How would I tell him of his daughter's decision to take holy vows?

Fearchar saw me and approached.

"Muirteach," he said, his blue eyes sparkling. "It is good to see you. It has been too long. And so how are things on Colonsay? You were sending that message and Mariota was all for coming to take care of it all herself—where is she, by the by?"

"She stayed on Colonsay," I answered foolishly.

"Did she indeed?" asked her father. "When is she meaning to return to Islay?"

"I think you will need to be asking her yourself."

"Indeed?" The Beaton looked at me with those piercing blue eyes of his, eyes so like his own daughter's. "Well, you must be explaining a bit of it all to me so that I am knowing the right questions to be asking her. Come along, and let us be going to my house across the causeway."

He looked around the great hall critically. The feast was well underway, and the MacRuaris were not the only men in their cups that gray afternoon. The MacInnes and my uncle had started a gambling match in one corner, and it looked to be a long evening.

"I am thinking folk here will have little need of a physician tonight. It is on the morrow that they will be having some aching heads. Unless some of these young *amadans* are drawing blood during the evening." Fearchar sighed, philosophical. "They will be sending for me if they are needing me."

I followed the Beaton across the causeway that led to the mainland from the Lord's castle, and into his neat house. I had first met Mariota in this very house earlier this year, before the events that had so grievously wounded her spirit.

Fearchar offered me some ale and added some peat to the embers smoldering on the hearth. In a short while we were seated cozily enough before a glowing fire, with the good smell of the burning peat surrounding us.

"And so, Muirteach, what of my daughter?" asked the Beaton with interest. "Where is she and when is she returning home? For I do confess I miss her sorely when she is not here."

This was growing worse and worse. I did not know how to break the news to him kindly, and ended by blurting it out.

"Mariota is with the nuns. Up at Cill Chaitrìona's near Balnahard."

"Indeed?" said her father again. "I am not altogether surprised by this."

I looked at him. My relief must have shown in my eyes.

"You are not?"

"No, lad, I am not. I am not such an unobservant old fool as my daughter takes me for—no, no, Muirteach, do not deny it. She has not been able to confide in me for fear of worrying me, but I have my own eyes, and I have seen how she is. I have seen this sort of thing before after people have gone through some great trials. Their humors are unbalanced and life is hard for them, sometimes for a long while."

I nodded and took a sip of my ale. "She was saying something of the sort. How she startles easily, does not wish to be alone, and yet she is unnerved by the noise of many people. She was saying she felt safe at the nunnery," I added bitterly. "Because of the walls and the quiet. She is not feeling safe with me."

"Muirteach, you are aye hard on yourself," observed Mariota's father. "You saved her life, and I am in your debt for that."

"There was something else as well," I added, relieved to speak of it with him. "We visited an old witch on Jura, and she was telling Mariota she would never make a healer. I think that discouraged her as well."

"And who was it you went to see?"

"Her name is Gormal. She is a crazy old *amadain* who lives in a cave on the west side of the island. That Benbecula MacDonald's wife had heard of her and went to have her scry to find out what had happened to young Niall. And then when Mariota heard of our visit, she wanted to go and see her. She said she had heard the woman had a remedy for the falling sickness, and she wanted to know of it."

"That would be my Mariota. I am knowing little of Gormal, although I have visited her—a long while since. I do not think the woman is from Jura, but she settled on the island many years ago. She does know a few remedies, but I am thinking she does not have the Sight, and my daughter was foolish herself indeed to be taking the old woman's words to heart in such a way. Do not be worrying so," he added, as he saw my expression, which must have given away more than I would have liked. "I am not thinking my daughter will make a nun."

"She was saying she wants to take her vows," I told him.

"Well, that would be some time from now, I am thinking," said her father calmly. "She will have ample time to consider. And if living in the nunnery truly will bring her peace, well, that is what I would wish for her."

"Aye," I muttered miserably. "I do wish her all happiness. And peace."

The Beaton changed the subject. "And what of these other matters? The bones you found and the murdered boy?"

"Niall was killed with a faerie arrow. But I am not thinking the *sithichean* were to blame. And Mariota thought the bones were those of an infant—some girl in trouble, I suppose, but no one seems to know anything about that at all, at all. To hear them, all the girls on Colonsay are paragons of the greatest virtue. And now there has been yet more trouble."

I told him of Liam's accident, the faerie gold, and the death of the child at Riasg Buidhe.

"So an innocent child sick with some fever died. And someone else on the island has found gold there and is killing because of it," mused the Beaton. "Well, it is not the first time that men have killed for gold."

"Aye, but to shoot a child in the back—"

"Indeed. That is a sad, sad thing. As is the death of the other poor boy."

Fearchar paused a moment, and I thought with a sudden pang of Niall's poor mangled body. Then my mind filled with images of the faerie trial I had seen at Riasg Buidhe. Surely the two deaths could not be connected. The boy at the village had been ill and died of it, while Niall's back had been pierced with an arrow. There was no relation. But I said nothing to the Beaton while I sat by his fire, thinking on it all.

The Beaton then continued, more briskly, "There is much evil in the world as you well know, Muirteach. And Niall's death must be related to the gold. But the poor village child . . . what profit would his death bring to anyone?"

I admitted that I saw none.

"Now," considered Fearchar, "about Niall's death. It can not be Liam for he would not be attacking himself, not in such a way as you've described. And you are not thinking it is the MacRuaris—why not again?"

"They truly seemed shocked when they heard of Liam's accident."

"Yes, but any man can act. What of the islanders? That Gillean or that Eachann?"

"I do not think they would be using faerie arrows," I said. "Nor do I think the MacRuaris would use them."

The Beaton nodded. "Someone would have to have a source

for them or know how to make them. And I do not think most men have that skill."

"Does any man?" I asked.

The Beaton thought. "There might be a few men, outlaws most likely, living in the wilds who might use flint points. If they can not get the iron points for arrows through trade, or some other way."

"I do not think there are such men on Colonsay," I said bitterly. "It is a small island, with no outlaws hiding in the hills."

"Perhaps not," agreed the Beaton.

We gazed at the embers for a time without speaking.

"What will you do about Mariota?" I finally asked. "Will you go and try and fetch her back?"

The Beaton chuckled oddly. "No, Muirteach, I am thinking I will not. Mariota can stay there as long as she needs to. I think that will be the best. Perhaps after a bit of time there, she will want to return to the world."

He looked at me, and I fancied I could see his love for his daughter on his face. "Mariota has always been headstrong, Muirteach. There was nothing like forbidding her something when she was a lass to ensure she would do it. And so, no, I think it will be best to leave her there with the good sisters for a while. I shall not interfere with her."

"And so you are back to Colonsay tomorrow, with your uncle?" he asked, after another pause.

I nodded.

"Well, Godspeed to you then, and a safe voyage. Why do you not bide here tonight? You will sleep better than over at the hall," Fearchar offered.

I was about to decline, thinking I was wanting to go back to the hall and get drunk on *uisgebeatha,* but then I surprised myself by accepting his offer. And I did sleep well and soundly in Fearchar's house, although perhaps my dreams were of his daughter. But I let those dreams linger gently in my mind, and did not speak of them to anyone.

Gillespic and I arrived back in Colonsay late the next afternoon after a slow sail home. A gale had sprung up against us, and the crew had to strain at the oars all the way across the sound in a wet soaking rain, all the more bitter for the November cold. One of the crew, a cousin of Fergus, was from up near the Tràigh Bàn, and we got to talking while we pulled in tandem at the oars.

"Old Àine raised you, did she not?"

The man Iain nodded.

"She is aye forgetful now."

Iain nodded again. "Were you knowing, Muirteach, that she was not even recognizing me last week when I was up there. And I raised by her like her own son. Old age is a sad thing indeed."

I agreed that it was.

"She is a kind woman, though," I added, and told Iain how she had taken me in that day I was returning from Balnahard. "And she brews a good ale. She knows many stories of the old days, for all that she did not remember my name."

"Aye, she does," agreed Iain, and we pulled at the oars in silence for a while.

"She was speaking to me of the faerie lights she sees on the hills above the Tràigh Bàn. Were you ever seeing those?" I asked Iain. Apparently he had, for he suddenly became less talkative.

"*Dia*, I do not wish to be speaking of them, not here out on the sea," replied Iain stubbornly. "Muirteach, you are a fool for sure to be bringing them up in such a way."

"You have the right of it," I said, hastening to change the subject. "I do not know what I was thinking. But old Àine remembers everything. Who were the people who lived up near the Beinn Beag?"

Iain thought for awhile. "I remember a woman lived there with her parents and a child. But I was young when they left."

"Where did they go?"

Iain shrugged his shoulders. "How should I know? I was just a child. The lad who lived up there was strange. They said the faeries took them all away, and I would believe it." Iain crossed himself, then swore. "Och, Muirteach, you have got me speaking of them again. I will say no more about them at all. Not until we are home and I am holding iron in my hands." And this time he did not speak of the faeries again.

CHAPTER 14

I stopped by Aorig's after we reached Scalasaig to retrieve my dog. Aorig claimed she was glad to have Somerled leave, although apparently he had been relatively well behaved the days I had been gone. He had only stolen one cheese and little Sean, at least, was sorry to see the dog go.

"I am wanting a dog of my own, Muirteach," he cried, the freckles on his nose squeezing together as tears welled up in his hazel eyes. "A puppy, like Somerled."

"Somerled is no puppy, Sean. Look at the great dog he is grown into."

"Aye, but I want a puppy of my own."

I found I was strangely unwilling to disappoint my half brother and felt suddenly bad for taking Somerled away from him.

"Well, we shall have to see. Perhaps my uncle's bitch will be having a litter soon."

Behind Sean I could see Aorig violently shaking her head no.

"But I do not think she is breeding," I amended hastily. "You will just have to be coming to Islay to visit the dog some day when I am back over there. It is a fine farm I have there now." Although the thought of my lands on Islay did not hold the same attraction they once did, when I knew Mariota Beaton to be living nearby.

"Why not come in and sit for awhile, Muirteach," invited Aorig. "I have some good fresh bannocks and can give you some ale to go with them."

I agreed that sounded like a fine thing and was soon settled by Aorig's hearth, watching the cheerful glow of the peat fire with a beaker of her fine-tasting ale. Aorig, of course, had heard of Mariota's going up to Balnahard and wished to speak of it, although I myself found the topic gave me little pleasure.

"I am not knowing why she wanted to go, Aorig. She was saying she felt safe up there, enclosed by those walls." I scowled at my ale a moment.

"Safe? From what?"

I scowled harder. "I am not knowing exactly."

"Perhaps," Aorig suggested, "what happened last summer was harder on her than she would admit."

"Aye, she was saying something of the sort. I am an *amadan*, Aorig. It was I put her life in danger last summer."

"And saved it again, Muirteach."

"No, she was simply running away when she had the chance."

"Well," said Aorig briskly, "I am thinking she would not have had her chance without you being there. And then she would have been over the cliff with that madman." She crossed herself quickly. "Thanks to God and his saints that that was not happening."

"Indeed," I concurred, but kept frowning at my ale.

"Muirteach, do you miss her that much?" Aorig laughed. "She has only been up there a few days."

"I do not miss her at all," I denied, and was about to rise to leave when I thought to ask her of the woman who had lived on the Beinn Beag. My ale was not quite finished. And the dark had set in by now outside.

"Were you ever hearing of a woman up on the Beinn Beag who was taken by the *sithichean?*" I asked. "With a child? A long while ago it would have been."

"I am not knowing, Muirteach. I do not have kin up there.

How did you hear of the matter?"

When I said that old Àine had told me of it, Aorig laughed again. "Her mind is going, Muirteach. I think the whole island knows of that! Poor old woman. I am thinking I must send Seamus over to the Tràigh Bàn with something for the poor old *amadain,* but I would not be trusting her stories overmuch."

I agreed with Aorig and when she asked me to have another glass of ale, I accepted with pleasure. My half brothers and half sister seemed happy enough living there with Aorig and her husband and Seamus. As I sat there listening to their chatter and the bustle of the family while Aorig got their supper together, I wondered what it would be like to have a wife and a family of my own. But that, I realized suddenly, was not like to happen, not with things the way they were now.

The cheerful bustle of the blackhouse suddenly oppressed me, and it was not long before I gathered Somerled up, made my excuses and left to make the lonely climb up to my uncle's dun in the bleak darkness of that November night. My bad leg pained me the whole way.

I arrived at the dun to find the evening meal nearly completed and my aunt awaiting me anxiously.

"Och, Muirteach, we were not sure where you had gone off to after himself and the others were arriving back from the boat."

"I stopped by Aorig's," I explained. "Somerled was there."

Strangely, I felt vindicated to know that my theory about Niall's death was probably correct. There was gold on the island, Niall had found it, and gotten in the way of someone else who had wanted it badly—badly enough to kill a young child for it. But who was that person?

Whoever the murderer was had used an faerie arrow with his bow. Very few islanders would dare to use faerie arrows; it was a brave man who would even pick one up for fear of getting elf-shot. Although as a young boy I had found one and kept it, carrying it in my sack of little treasures. And had feared later that it had given me my limp after the fever took me as a small boy. That had been a short while before my mother had died of the Black Death, long before I had seen the Isle of Colonsay. We had lived on Islay then.

But those musings did not answer the question of Niall's faerie arrow. Who would use such a thing besides the *sithichean*? And the *sithichean* did not usually kill their victims with a bloody wound in the back. That was a human trait.

The killer would have to be someone who had no fear of the faerie. Or perhaps someone who lived on the fringes of society, who had no access to iron tips for his arrows. I thought of Gillean, that old man who lived by himself up there by the Carnan Eoin. Although he had said he had thrown the gold bracelet into the lochan, perhaps he was not as innocent as he seemed.

Or perhaps Liam had killed Niall for the gold and then been thrown from his horse. But if that had been the case, where was the gold now? It certainly had not been found near Liam.

Perhaps Gillean, or whoever had taken the gold, had found Liam with the gold and then attacked him. Aye, and perhaps it was old Àine herself, I told myself hopelessly. It did not seem likely to me that a frail old woman had hit Liam over the head with a rock and then stolen his gold. But then, I did not really believe old Gillean had done that either, although I wondered about the death of the child at the village. But that boy had been sick and died of it. Children sickened and died far too often.

And what of the poor little bones in the cave, and the story of the woman and her child taken by the faerie on Beinn Beag? Perhaps the bones were those of that child. The saints alone knew what had happened to its mother—or perhaps the *sithich-*

ean knew, if they had indeed taken her, and the saints were knowing nothing of it at all, at all.

But now I had seen some of the gold myself, and knew that at least part of my speculations were true. I resolved to visit Gillean again the next day to see if I could glean anything more about his possible involvement in the two disasters. I cursed myself for a shortsighted fool after making this resolution, to be so suspicious of a poor old man. But my cursing did not deter my questions, and I mulled over the possibility of his guilt as I downed some more of my aunt's good ale.

The next morning I set out for Gillean's. The sun rose late this time of the year and was just peeking over the mountains as I started out. The air was chill and crisp, the sky a pale light blue, like the little blue of the wildflowers on the *machair* in the summer. There had been a frost the night before, and each blade of grass was outlined in its icy coating of tiny crystals.

The chill in the air caused me to hurry the horse a bit, but before I reached Gillean's I saw one of the sisters from Cill Chaitríona on the hills nearby. She looked to be behaving strangely, running wildly over the land in what seemed to me a very odd fashion for a nun.

I was sorely tempted to ignore her and pass the other way. I wanted no part of those sisters and feared speaking or seeing one of them would put me in mind of Mariota all over again, and I had other concerns to deal with today. But I began to worry that perhaps the poor woman had hurt herself or some such thing, to be acting in such a fey fashion. So I turned the horse in her direction and approached her.

I drew nearer and recognized her with surprise, for it was the younger of the two sisters I had seen so many weeks ago gathering their herbs. Morag, I remembered Mariota had called her.

"Sister Morag!"

The woman turned to look at me like a hare about to dart away.

"Is it hurt you are, then?" I asked her, reining in my horse.

She shook her head no. Her wimple was disheveled and askew, showing a bit of cropped dark hair. She wore no *brat*, just her nun's robes, and as I watched her I saw her feet were bare, even in the cold. She must have just run outside without dressing for the weather or the chill of the morning. Her eyes looked red, and I could see wetness and tear stains on her cheeks. Even a fool, such as I was when it came to the ways of women, could surmise that she had been crying.

"Can I be helping you? What is it that is wrong? Where are the other sisters?"

She shook her head in answer to my first question, then began to laugh wildly. Her laughter had a crazed and wild sound to it, putting me in mind of the madman from last summer, and I began to grow a little afeared of what she might do.

"It is cold you are. Have you no shoes?"

She shook her head no again.

"Shouldn't you be going back to Cill Chaitríona? The other sisters will be aye worried for you. Here. You can ride on my horse, and I will take you there."

At this the woman darted away, but I followed her quickly enough on my horse and then dismounted. She tried again to run, but I grabbed her arm and when she felt my grip, for I do have good strength in my arms, she stopped struggling and stood quietly enough. I looked down and saw her feet, red with cold, against the white frost-rimmed leaves of grass.

"Look you," I said, becoming annoyed with the good sisters in general and with this one in particular, "I am unwilling to leave you here to freeze. Why, I do not know. But there it is. So you will be coming with me now, and I will take you to Cill Chaitríona. Now get on my horse."

147

And surprisingly, she did so, without resisting me. I sat her in front of me, and we rode the short distance up to Cill Chaitriona. I saw her shoulders shaking with quiet sobs as we rode, but I did not know why she cried.

It was soon enough we reached the nunnery and the gatekeeper came running out to meet us, followed by the abbess.

"Sister Morag," Abbess Bride said, scolding her as you would scold a child, "You must be coming inside. It's a fine lot of worry and bother you've caused us today."

I must have looked puzzled, for the abbess turned towards me. "It is Muirteach, is it not? The same one who is working for His Lordship?"

I nodded in assent.

"You seem to be making a habit of bringing women to our doors and leaving them," she added, with a wry touch of humor I had not seen before in her. "Sister Morag has caused us great worry with her behavior, and we must thank you for returning her to us."

"She seems upset over something. Are you knowing what it might be?"

Abbess Bride shook her head. "Indeed I am not knowing. You need have no concerns for her," she continued, effectively dismissing me. "Sister Morag will be fine now that she is back among us, and we shall take steps to ensure she does not wander again."

That sounded somewhat sinister. I felt at a bit of a loss as to how to proceed, but I bethought myself of my years at the priory, and the lessons I learned there helped me a bit the now.

"Mother, I rejoice to have restored the poor sister to you. Still, I am gravely concerned for the woman's health. Might I speak with your infirmarian, to apprise her of the sad condition I found the poor sister in? I would wish for the Lord of the

Isles, when next I see him, to know all is well here at Cill Chai-triona."

Abbess Bride did not look overly pleased at this, but she did not deny me. "Very well," she said, with a tight, pursed look to her lips. She brought me to the same small stone room Fergus and I had visited some weeks before, and I heard her send for Sister Euphemia.

I did not wait long this time before I heard the sound of footsteps outside. A measured tread and a lighter, faster step I fancied I recognized.

"Muirteach, it is you!" Mariota burst into the room.

"Mo chridhe!" I forgot myself and clasped her in my arms and she did not resist. Just for a moment it was, until we remembered ourselves and disentangled, as Sister Euphemia glared at us disapprovingly. But Mariota's elderflower scent lingered in my senses, and I returned the sister's glare with a smile.

"Sister Euphemia, this is Muirteach, whom I was speaking of."

"Indeed." Sister Euphemia continued glaring at me. "We have met before. You were looking into the death of that poor lad who was slain by the *sithichean.*" She made the sign of the cross.

It seemed the nunnery, for all its isolation, received its share of the news.

"Indeed, Sister, that was the way of it. And was I not bringing Mariota here as well? She is like a sister to me," I lied, still feeling a little guilty about our stolen embrace.

"Indeed?" repeated Sister Euphemia.

I felt it best not to pursue that topic.

"I was riding out towards old Gillean's this morning," I said, "and found poor Sister Morag, wandering in the cold like a poor *amadain.* I returned her here and wanted to tell you of what I found."

"Yes?"

"The sad thing seemed aye distressed, in tears. At first it seemed she did not want to return here. But then she came willingly enough. I am concerned. You would not be knowing what has bothered her so?"

"Indeed and I am not. Nor am I thinking it need concern you."

"Perhaps not. But she seemed overwrought. And I have been investigating the death on the island—that young Niall—and then that accident with that man from Mull."

"Aye. One of the shepherds was bringing news of that, just yesterday it was."

"And so I wondered if this might in some way relate?"

"I can not think so," said Sister Euphemia, relenting a bit. "Sister Morag knew nothing of the man from Mull or that poor lad. But I am not knowing why she would run away in such a fashion. She has been here some five years. She is a good enough sister and helps me with the herbs."

"So you are knowing her well?"

"As well as any here do. Sister Morag was a flighty girl when first she came to us, but she has gained maturity in her years here. I confess I am worried about her."

"As I am. Well, thank you for your help."

Sister Euphemia turned to leave, followed by Mariota who had been uncharacteristically silent during our speech. Perhaps this was due to her status in the nunnery, I thought.

"Sister," I asked before they left the room. "Might I not converse a bit with Mariota here, just out in the cloisters?"

"As she is thinking of leaving the world behind her, I can not think you would have much to speak of," said Sister Euphemia sternly. "But she has not taken any vows." She considered, and suddenly Sister Euphemia relented. Her hazel eyes twinkled a little, and I thought I saw the beginnings of a smile on her lips. "Very well. You may walk in the outer courtyard and I will walk behind you. But no brotherly embraces, young man."

I could feel the blush rise in my cheeks and felt like a lad caught out stealing from the kitchen, but was pleased to get a chance to speak with Mariota for all of that. I followed Sister Euphemia and Mariota willingly enough to the small courtyard, where Sister Euphemia promptly seated herself on a bench and Mariota and I could finally speak together.

"And how is it with you, *mo chridhe?*" I asked. "Are you well?"

"Well enough," said Mariota. "I can sleep well here, at least. It is safe here."

"That is good," I said awkwardly. "I have missed you."

"And I you." The silence lingered a moment while we walked, then Mariota changed the subject in that brisk way she had.

"I was spending quite a bit of time with Sister Morag, Muirteach."

"Aye?"

"Yes. And I am thinking perhaps she knew Liam MacLean better than she had cause to."

"Was she confiding in you?"

"Not exactly." Mariota frowned a bit, and spoke in an undertone to me. "But she would frequently make excuses to go out gathering herbs. She liked to go alone, would be gone for hours, and have little enough to show in her basket when she returned. I suppose she could have met him in the hills. And when the shepherd came yesterday with the news about Liam— for I had said nothing of it here myself—she went all pale. I saw her bite her lip until the blood came. Then last night when we were to be sleeping, I heard what sounded like sobs from her pallet. And then this morning, she was gone."

We heard Sister Euphemia cough warningly from her bench.

"I must go, Muirteach. But I will try to find out more."

"And send word to me?" I asked, mockingly. For a nunnery is not the easiest place to communicate from.

"I have taken no vows," said Mariota, a little defiantly. "I will send a letter. If I can."

"Aye, *mo chridhe*. That will do fine."

And then Mariota was whisked away by Sister Euphemia, and I was left to find my own way out to my patiently waiting horse.

CHAPTER 15

I left the nunnery, riding hard until I reached Lochan Gammhich and Gillean's cottage. After all, he had been my original reason for setting out that day, although in all the confusion with the wandering Sister Morag I had nearly forgotten about him. The blue smoke of his peat fire curled up out of the thatching and looked cozy enough to me, for the day had not warmed much. I dismounted and called to him.

He appeared at the door flap, looking a bit confused, but his face cleared as he saw me.

"And it is you yourself. How have you been faring, young Muirteach? I was thinking you might have been returning to Islay by now."

I shook my head no. "I am staying here the while. Himself on Islay is wanting to find out who was after harming that MacLean that was found here."

"The man fell from his horse," insisted Gillean. "Well, it is a cold enough day. You must come in, and have some *uisgebeatha* to warm yourself. And perhaps a bite of porridge."

I agreed readily enough, and was soon seated before Gillean's fire. We spoke of the weather for a while and after exhausting that and other topics, I finally asked what I really wished to know.

"And so, have you seen more faerie lights? Or found more gifts from the *sithichean?*"

Gillean crossed himself and reached for the protective iron of his dirk.

"No, Muirteach. I am thinking they are satisfied now, with that young boy they have taken. And the other as well, the poor lad from Riasg Buidhe. No, they have been quiet. But what with the bad weather, I am thinking they are safe and warm in the *sithean,* feasting and enjoying their treasure. And those poor young lads are with them there as well, their prisoners."

Having seen Niall's poor body, I did not think he was with the *sithichean.* But the fact that his body had been found apparently made no difference to Gillean.

"Although they say," he continued, thoughtfully, "that time is as nothing to them in their faerie hills. So perhaps that young Niall thinks he has just been there for a moment."

"Perhaps," I said, not knowing how else to reply. "And have you found any more of their treasure?"

"No indeed." Gillean took another swig of *uisgebeatha.* "But I was finding something else they were leaving."

"And what was that?"

"Some faerie weapons. Here, I will show them to you."

Gillean rose from his seat near the smoking fire and went over to a rough chest near the wall. He opened it and withdrew a package wrapped in a sheepskin. The sheepskin stank.

"Here it is. Now, you must be saying nothing of it to anyone. For I am not wanting the *sithichean* to know I have been stealing from them. Or I will be getting into trouble with them for sure."

I promised I would keep quiet about whatever it was he had found, for Gillean still had not unwrapped the parcel to show me.

"Aye, well, that is good enough then," the old man said after I had sworn a promise on his iron dirk. He proceeded, with agonizing slowness, to unwrap his parcel. Inside was an arrow, tipped with a worked flint point.

"An arrow," I said. "Where were you finding it?"

"It is not an arrow," insisted Gillean, who I was beginning to realize was quite a stubborn man. "It will be one of their faerie spears. They are not tall enough to be shooting an arrow of this size from a bow."

"Perhaps not."

"Their arrows will be smaller, like a dart," Gillean explained. "Which is why you are not always knowing when it is that you are struck. That young boy was killed with a faerie spear. That is what I was hearing. Is it true?" he asked me suddenly. "You were finding the body."

I agreed that that must have been the way of it.

"Might I examine this?" I asked.

"I would be feeling better about it if you had some iron on you. Do you?"

I showed him my own dirk.

"Aye, I suppose there can be no harm in it then," agreed Gillean.

"And why were you keeping this and not throwing it back into the lochan for them as well?" I asked as I looked at the arrow.

Gillean shrugged his shoulders. "I will have to be giving it back to them soon, I am guessing. But the weather was not so fine, and my joints were paining me. And so I did not want to make the walk up to that little lochan, not in this bad weather. I am thinking they have more weapons."

I agreed with him and examined the arrow more closely. The shaft was willow, fletched with hawk feathers. The point itself was of crudely worked flint, attached with sinew. Aside from the point, it did not look so strange. The point closely resembled the one we had found in Niall's back, but something else about it nagged at my mind. Surely no one on the island worked flint?

That was a faerie skill. We used iron for arrow tips, although I supposed if someone was so poor as to have no iron, they might be using flint.

"They say you are a faerie doctor. How is it you are knowing so much about the faerie spears and arrows? And knowing how to drive away the *sithichean* out of people?" I asked Gillean as I put the arrow aside on its sheepskin and settled back by the fire. I took another gulp of *uisgebeatha*.

"Och, it is just that I am living alone here. And I learned much of it from my dam. She was a wise woman, for all that she was not kind to me. People would be calling on her for help with many things. But she died many years ago."

"And do people often call on you for help with the *sithichean?*"

"Not often. I am just a poor old man living alone in the hills. But I remember some of what my mother taught me."

"But your mother was not knowing how to work the flint?"

"No, no, only the *sithichean* are knowing that." Gillean took another swallow, then said confidingly, "When I was a young boy, though, we played at it. Working the flint. We found some over by the Uamh Ur, and we would play at striking pieces of it with other rocks to make knives and such. Then my mother found us, and she was aye angry. She said the *sithichean* would be stealing us away for playing with such things."

"But they did not."

"They were not stealing me," agreed Gillean, "for they had already taken me when I was just a babe. I was telling you that story already. That is part of the reason I am thinking they will not be too angered if I keep the spear a wee while until I can make the climb up to that lochan to give it back to them."

"Who did you play with? What other boys from the island?"

"That Eachann, the one that is still living here. And Mànus, and Calum. We were boys together many, many years ago it is now. And others, but they are all gone now. They were taken long ago."

"They died?"

"Many died in the plague." Gillean set down the jug of *uisge-beatha*. "It was taking Calum, and Mànus. Grown men we all were then, though. And it took my own mother, although she was old enough at that time."

"Aye. It took my own mother as well," I answered, feeling suddenly melancholy. It must have been the drink in me.

"She was cruel to me, my mother," continued Gillean. "And I was cruel to her in my turn. I used to call her an old fool before the plague took her. She was getting so old that she could not do for herself, but was needing me to help her as if she was a baby. I had to feed her, and wipe her wrinkled old bum. And I did care for her, indeed I did, although she was not thanking me for it. No, not a word of thanks did I get from the old bitch." Gillean took another swig of *uisgebeatha,* then continued. "She was always saying that she wished the *sithichean* had been keeping me, instead of that other one. It was hard she was to me, my mother."

"What other one was that?"

"She would have been speaking of that boy who was taken by the faeries. With his mother. They lived over on the Beinn Beag."

I remembered Àine saying something of that earlier.

"What happened to them?"

"It was just as I was telling you. Were you not listening?" Gillean put the flask down and looked at me, annoyed. "Must I be telling you again?"

I begged his pardon and the old man continued.

"The *sithichean* took them both one night. The woman's parents were saying the young boy was a changeling and were giving him the herbs to eat to drive the faerie out of him. My mother helped them, for she knew of such things. They forced the herbs into him for days, it was. But the herbs were not working, and that night the *sithichean* were coming and stealing the both of them, the mother and the son. Aye, it was a grand host of the *sithichean,* right enough. They came riding their fine faerie horses, all dressed in green and red silks."

"Were you seeing them, then?"

"No, it was not I that saw them. It was the woman's own parents who spoke of it. And my mother was there with them and saw them as well. They had put the lad to the fire to drive the changeling out of him. But the changeling would not leave. And all of a sudden wasn't there a fearsome rush of wind all around their house and a wild wailing, and there were the hosts of the *sithichean* outside with the bridles of their horses jingling with the silver and all glowing with a silver, fey light. And then they were taking the changeling up with them along with the mother, for she was a handsome woman and one of the faerie lords was taking a fancy to her. So they took the woman with them as well, and were they not going back to their faerie hills— the ones that are over on the monks' island. And neither the woman nor the child have been seen again to this day. But they are living still in the *sithean,* feasting and dancing there with the faerie lords.

"Indeed," continued Gillean, who had now warmed to his story, "perhaps they are not even knowing how many years have passed here in our world. Perhaps it is only a day for them."

"Perhaps," I agreed, attempting to stifle a yawn. Gillean had a fine talent for long-windedness, I was discovering. "Well, I thank you for your kindness and for the drink. But the day is growing short, and I must be heading back down the island."

Gillean nodded. "You will be wanting to get home before it is dark, indeed. You will not be wanting to run into the hosts of them riding out from their faerie hills. Are you having some iron with you, then?"

I assured him again that I did, and then I set off, back towards Dun Evin as the sun set, a red sinking ball in the west over the Tràigh Bàn.

I managed to reach the dun without encountering the *sithichean,* not that I was truly expecting to be meeting up with them. Still, I found that Gillean's stories had made me uneasy, as if I would not be uneasy enough with a murderer loose on the island. A murderer who worked flint.

And it was interesting to learn that both Eachann and Gillean both had experimented with making flint knives and such, as lads.

And what of Sister Morag? Surely she was no flint-worker. Neither was Liam. I had seen his bow, and he had had fine arrows, tipped with steel. Although his fine bow had not helped him in the end.

Well, perhaps Mariota would be learning something more about Sister Morag, and somehow getting word of it to me. Although I doubted she would have much opportunity to send messages from the nunnery, I did not doubt Mariota's resourcefulness. I wondered again, for perhaps the thousandth time, if her father was right about her. Perhaps she would not stay with the nuns. It had felt fine to hold her in my arms again, even so briefly, at Cill Chaitrìona. I found myself reliving that stolen kiss in my aunt's storeroom more often than I cared to admit.

I wondered what had happened to the woman and child from Beinn Beag that Gillean and Àine had spoken of. Although there were tales of people being stolen by the faerie all over the islands, it was seldom enough that I had heard of people being taken here, on this island. With that in mind, I sought out my aunt, who was in the kitchen overseeing preparations for the evening meal.

"Och, Muirteach, I could not be saying. You know I am from

Tiree, and it was not until I was marrying your uncle that I was coming to this island. And I am thinking, if it happened indeed, it was long before that time. We have only been married for seventeen years." Euluasaid turned her attention to the kitchen. "You, Tormod, help Marsali with the meats over there. She is having all she can do to see to it on her own."

My aunt turned to me again and continued, "I have heard tales, of course, of the *sithichean*. And that they were seen on the Beinn Beag. And wasn't that just the reason I was so afrightened when Niall went missing." For a second my aunt looked ready to cry again, and I felt ashamed for asking her about the matter, but she controlled herself and went on speaking. "We are almost ready to eat, Muirteach. I am thinking you will be hungry after your long day on the north of the island. How did Mariota seem to you? Was she looking well?"

Truth to tell, I was ravenous, and the good smells of bannocks and rabbit stew coming from the kitchen hall increased my desire for food. So I did not puzzle more on the stolen woman and child at that time, but reassured my aunt that Mariota indeed had seemed well. Then I took my place at the table, filled my trencher, and sated my hunger for a spell. However I sat next to Fergus, Àine's nephew, and thought to ask him about the stolen mother and child as we drank a last bit of ale before leaving the feast.

Fergus was older than I. He had taught me the little I knew of hunting and had kept me under his wing a bit when I first came there, a newly motherless lad from Islay so long ago. I looked at the bit of gray in his hair and realized with a little shock that he was growing older.

"A woman and child stolen by the faerie on Beinn Beag." He thought for a moment, then set down the beaker. "Aye, I am remembering that. Who was telling you of it? My auntie?"

"Aye, and old Gillean was speaking of it as well."

"Yes, I remember well. They lived up on the Beinn Beag—you can still see the bit of their house standing there, in the circle of stones upon the hill. The lad was a strange one. He did not speak much, but he would come along with us sometimes when we played."

"When was all of this happening?"

"It was long ago. I was a lad, about eleven. So that would make it close to twenty-four years gone that it was happening."

I had not even been born yet.

"Do you think he was a changeling?" I asked Fergus abruptly.

"The lad? Aye, he could well have been. He was a strange one. He did not speak and would stare at things for hours. He was fey."

"How so?"

"He would sit for hours and count limpet shells. Over and over he would count them. We used to tease him about it, Mànus and I. But Mànus is gone now. The Black Death was taking him ten years ago."

"But what happened to the boy?"

"It is as Gillean was telling you. He and his mother both disappeared one night. And the boy's grandparents were saying they had been stolen by the *sithichean,* and who was I to be disbelieving them." Fergus stopped and crossed himself. "The boy's grandparents had been trying to drive the faerie out of the lad for some time. I remember my own mother speaking of it. You know how the women talk. But the *sithichean* came and took the changeling back and stole his mother as well. They vanished and were not seen again after that night by anyone."

"What happened to the grandparents?"

"They lived there, on the Beinn Beag. Until the plague took them."

"And how were they called?"

Fergus looked confused. "The old grandparents?"

"Well, I was meaning the woman and the child."

"He had a strange name, with an L it was, it was not Lachlan—no, no, he was called Lulach."

"And his mother?"

"I am thinking she was called Gormlaith."

"That witch on Jura is called Gormal. That is not so different."

Fergus looked skeptical. "I am not thinking they moved to Jura. That is not what the grandparents said about it all. They said they were stolen by the *sithichean.*"

"Perhaps they lied," I suggested.

"What reason would they have to do that?" asked Fergus reasonably. "No, Muirteach, I am thinking they truly were stolen by the faerie." He spat and crossed himself.

"Perhaps," I agreed, as we finished the last of our ale. "Come, let's play chess."

I managed to beat Fergus at chess, not without some difficulty. It was at first hard for me to concentrate on the game, as my mind was full of what I had learned. Fergus had me in check a time or two, but eventually my concentration sharpened. At the last minute I was able to get him in checkmate. Fergus and my uncle had taught me chess, and I still felt some small pride on the occasions I was able to beat him.

But as we finished this game, my mind immediately went back to what Gillean and Fergus had told me and, refreshed by the game and my small triumph, I saw things a trifle differently. Suppose the young lad and his mother had not been stolen by the faerie but had simply left Colonsay. And then the grandparents had put out the story of them being stolen away to cover it up. Gillean's mother might not have wanted to admit that she had failed to drive out the changeling, so she might have told the same story. Aye, I thought cynically, perhaps that was true, but that still did not explain who had shot poor little

162

Niall or attacked Liam. For if the mother and child had left Colonsay twenty-four years ago, well then, they were not on the island. At least no one had seen them there.

But the distance between Jura and Colonsay is not so great. People can easily travel between the two islands. I had seen that Gormal had a boat. And Gormlaith and her son had lived on the Beinn Beag, near where the gold had been found by Gillean and by Niall. So perhaps Gormal was truly Gormlaith, and had known of the gold then and returned to find it. I had not seen gold at Gormal's house on Jura, but she seemed to live comfortably enough in her cave. If she had gold, she would not display it openly. And at that, I realized I would be going to Jura again, and very soon.

CHAPTER 16

I told Uncle Gillespic what I had in mind the next morning, and he listened intently to my theories.

"Aye, Muirteach, I am remembering a little of when that woman disappeared. It was a nine days' wonder on the island, but I was forgetting about the most of it long ago. It was mostly women's talk, I am thinking, but it is true enough that the woman vanished along with her child. I was but a lad. My father was still the chief at that time. I am thinking he thought she had run off with some lover and taken the child with her. He was no great believer in the *sithichean*."

"So you are not thinking that the Gormlaith who disappeared and the witch on Jura would be the same?"

My uncle shrugged his shoulders. "I am not knowing, Muirteach. But you are welcome to the *nabhaig* and a few men to help you crew it if you wish to visit that old witch woman again."

However the weather was not for us; a squall set in, and so we waited for several days while the hails and rains beat down upon the islands. Frustrated, I drank too much and went down to my house in Scalasaig accompanied by Somerled, for the cheerful clatter and activity of the dun began to oppress me. My house was a mess. I had paid little attention to it since the last summer; the roof was leaking worse than ever, and the few furnishings were covered with dust. I managed to get a small fire going in the hearth, and then I went to sleep. I dreamt of

Mariota and hordes of tall shining ones, silver *sithichean* bejeweled in faerie gold who dragged her away, out of my arms, and down into the depths of their faerie hills while she fought and cried against them. But I awoke to the same dreary leaking roof and the dark coldness of my house while Somerled slept on undisturbed. His dreams were only of rabbits.

Finally the weather cleared up enough for the trip to Jura, and Gillespic's *nabhaig* was prepared for the trip. Why he was willing to lend me boats I was not sure, but Gillespic was a generous soul. At least he had been so to me from the time he had taken me in as a small boy. I made my plans and enlisted Seamus again and Fergus, and along with one other man to help crew we set off the next morning for the Isle of Jura.

The wind was crisp and the crossing quick also, and we soon anchored at the small cove below Gormal's cave. I had brought gifts for her: some fine lengths of woolen cloth that I had convinced my aunt to part with, along with some cheeses and some meal. Gormal had not been overly friendly to me before, and I was hoping that these might placate her somewhat. But we took weapons along as well. For I was mindful of the mess I had made of things that last summer on Mull. And this time I was not so overconfident.

We climbed the path up the cave one more time. Gormal was there, although we saw no sign of her servant—or son. She answered the door, scowling a bit when she saw me.

"We have brought you some gifts," I said, "to make up for the trouble we have caused you in the past."

Gormal said nothing at first.

"Please, won't you be accepting them?"

"And what if I do?"

"We are just wanting to speak with you a bit. About the troubles over on our island."

"And what would I be knowing about that?" Gormal looked

at the men with me and shrugged, defeated. "You may as well come in, and you can be telling me the story."

And so we came inside and sat once more on her benches and gave her our gifts. She barely looked at them, but acknowledged them with some words of thanks.

"And now, what is it that is bringing you across the sound yet another time? I did not realize that the Colonsay men were such folk for sailing."

"Well," I started to speak, a little awkwardly, "it is just that we were hearing stories."

"Yes?"

"Stories of a woman from Colonsay with a boy, who disappeared many years ago. It is said that they were stolen by the *sithichean*."

"And what is that to me?"

"The woman was called Gormlaith."

"There are many women with that name. It is not so rare as all that."

"And it is not so different from your own name, as well. But this woman had a son. One who did not speak. It was thought he was a changeling."

I thought I saw a flicker of some emotion cross Gormal's face.

"I have no son. It was not me."

"No? And who is that man who helps you here?"

"A servant only."

"Truly?"

A golden eagle circled over the hills. I glimpsed it through the open door of the cave against the light blue of the sky. I watched it a moment without speaking.

"Sure, any mother would do much to save her child from being put to the fire. If it was her child, indeed, and not a changeling."

Gormal's face twisted. "But I did not save him," she said in an undertone. "I could not save him from that."

"Then where is he? Did he die?" I asked gently.

She shook her head. "No, he did not die. He is here. But the faerie never gave my own son back to me. Not even after I saved theirs when he was put to the fire. I have cared for the one they left me so long ago. I have guarded him carefully and tried to do everything for him just as they would want. And he grew into a strong one indeed. But they were never returning my true son to me, for all that I have tried to care for theirs all of these years."

"Let us see him," I said.

"Lulach. His name is Lulach. It was my son's name, and I kept it for their changeling."

"Let us see him," I repeated.

"He is off away. He is hunting. But he will return soon."

"Is he a sailor?"

"Aye. He knows how to use the boat. He fishes with it."

"Does he go as far as Colonsay with it?"

Gormal shrugged her shoulders again. "I've no way of knowing where it is that he goes. But true enough he will be going for several days, and then he is back again."

"Is he a good hunter?"

"Aye. Lulach is good with the bow. He keeps me well fed with the deer, and rabbit or birds as well when there are no deer to be found. Here," Gormal said, "I will just be getting you some ale to wet your throats while you are waiting for him."

She went to the back of her cave and soon brought us some ale in a four-sided wooden *mether*, to pass the one to the other. We had a thirst on us after the voyage, and drained the cup quickly, although the ale had a dark, earthy taste. A little bitter, still it was not unpleasant and quenched the thirst. She quickly refilled the *mether* and we sent it round again.

"Now," Gormal said. "We will just wait for him."

The peat fire smoked pleasantly warm against the chill of the afternoon and her house was snug and warm enough against the lowering darkness. The atmosphere grew stuffy, and I could not keep my eyes open. Too late I realized what must have happened, but that realization did me no good. As the knowledge sank in, I drifted deeper into some spell or strange slumber.

I was in the room, the same room, and yet powerless to move. A stag wandered in, but strangely, it had a man's eyes. I did not wonder overmuch at this, but I marveled at the rich softness of the brown fur and the deep darkness of the eyes. As I looked more closely into them, I realized they were like the eyes of Lulach. As I watched, he transformed into a man, then back into a stag and then left the room, which now seemed somehow to be full of twisting and writhing vines growing before my eyes, twisting and twining around my legs like a serpent. They held me rooted fast to my seat, so that I was powerless to move. I looked up and saw that the roof of the cave was gone. The ceiling was transparent, and above it were the stars glimmering in the heavens. Somehow then I was free to move, and I climbed up beams of light into the stars, feeling a mysterious joy in my heart and freedom in my limbs as I neared the crystal sparkling light of them. The light burst into my soul and then I felt myself falling back into the dark blackness of the cave, but with a strange sense of illumination shining in my being as I lost consciousness.

We awoke the next morning to the early winter sun streaming in through the open door of the witch's cave. My head was splitting with pain and as I glanced at the sunbeams, my stomach rolled. I ran outside and vomited.

The witch and her changeling son had vanished, like the

dreams of the night. The cave was empty, in some disarray, and it seemed that many things had been quickly gathered together in the night before they were leaving the place.

"Oh, my head," groaned Fergus as he staggered somewhat unsteadily back inside. "Sure and wasn't she outsmarting us, the *cailleach*."

"They have gone," reported a breathless Seamus, winded from running down to the cove and then back up the steep path. "Their small boat is gone."

"And ours?" I asked, remembering what had happened last summer when another boat of my uncle's had been sabotaged.

"It is still there where we beached it. It does not look disturbed," he added, his voice sharp with anxiety.

"Well, we will be inspecting it before we are sailing away in it. Do not worry, Seamus. It will be seaworthy."

"Where would they go to ground?" Seamus asked.

"Surely not back to Colonsay. No, now I am thinking they might just have sailed around the island here, to another bitty cave someplace. There are caves up by Corpach where they might be hiding. Now that we know who they are."

"Aye," agreed Fergus. "Well, there is nothing I would rather be doing today than to be hunting for that bitch and her changeling. My head is paining me something awful, indeed."

So we set out, spending that day and the next searching the many caves along the west coast of Jura for Gormal and her son. But we were not finding them.

We returned to Colonsay three days later, disheartened. The witch and her son had vanished. Perhaps, I thought, they had returned to the *sithean*, the faerie hills indeed, for we found no sight of them, nor of their small boat. After we gave up combing the coastline, we crossed the sound and finally saw the familiar bulk of Colonsay loom blackly in our vision as we pulled into the harbor at Scalasaig. We beached the boat and then, frustrated, I headed straight for Donald Dubh's, accompanied by Fergus. Seamus went with us happily enough, but the other man had a young wife waiting at home and quickly left us.

"Will not your mother be wanting to see you?" asked Fergus.

Seamus hesitated a moment. "Perhaps she will not be knowing the boat has put into the harbor. I will stay just a while and have some ale."

Seamus had worked as hard as any of us at the oars and the sailing. He had proved himself growing out of his youth and into his manhood, and so I did not wish to gainsay him his ale with us. We all filed into the alehouse through the rough hide door and settled ourselves on benches and stools by the glow of the peat fire.

Donald Dubh's wife brought us some ale and some *uisge-beatha,* and I for one was glad of the fire of the whiskey as it coursed down my throat. The thirst was on the men and on myself, and it was not taking me long to drink more than perhaps was wise. I was just relaxing in the warmth of the fire and of the drink when the door flap raised and in walked Aorig. Seamus saw her first.

"Mother—"

"There you are, Seamus. I was hearing you all had returned and was wanting to see you."

I looked to see if Aorig was angry; in the dim light of the tavern it was hard to be certain, but I though I saw a smile playing around the corners of her mouth. She did not look to be put out to find Seamus here. He was growing older, after all, and it was no secret that Aorig's husband spent enough of his time in this tavern as well.

"Well, and what is it?" asked Seamus a little defiantly.

"It was just that I was wanting to see with my own eyes you were home safe. No more than that, my son. No, it is Muirteach who might be wanting to stir himself and head up to Dun Evin. You are fine, son. Finish your ale, for I am thinking you have earned it these days."

"And why would I be wanting to head up to Dun Evin?" I asked Aorig.

"It is just that Mariota has returned from Cill Chaitrìona."

"She is back?" I said stupidly, wishing I had not drunk so much so quickly.

"Indeed she is," continued Aorig, smiling more broadly now. "And staying again with your aunt and uncle. But it is you she has been asking for."

I did not rush out of the tavern at these words, although part of me wished to fly like the wind up the hill to the dun. But I can not fly like the wind, and I limp.

Instead I finished my ale, not wanting to appear overeager, and bought another round for the crew as I settled up the bill. And then, finally, I rose and left the tavern, taking a torch with me. By the flicker of its light I slowly picked my way up the path to the dun, accompanied by Fergus.

My aunt and uncle were glad to see me, but I paid little heed to Euluasaid's warm words of greeting. Instead, my eyes roved the smoky darkness of the hall searching for Mariota. I did not find her at first, and I wondered if Aorig had been lying when she spoke. I sat down on a vacant bench near Gillespic and took a drink of ale, but all the time my mind was as flighty as a young colt, running this way and that in the pasture. Until finally I calmed enough to sense someone standing next to me. It was Mariota, holding a pitcher of ale.

"I was wondering, just, when you would see me," she said as my eyes met hers.

"I've a sad tendency to poor-sightedness." I felt awkward and tongue-tied, as though I spoke with someone I did not know.

"Are you wanting more ale?"

"That would be a fine thing. And yourself? Sit down and drink some with me."

Mariota did so, pouring the *mazer* full again for me, and took a sip of it herself. I looked at her sweet face and felt joy that she was no longer in Balnahard.

"And so you were leaving the nuns?" I asked after a moment when Mariota had not spoken.

A shadow crossed Mariota's face. "I fell out with the abbess. She felt I had a nature not submissive enough." I thought I saw an angry glint in her blue eyes, in the dim light of the hall, before she continued. "And I may burn in hell for it, but indeed I myself felt I was not as obedient as might be. Nor did I have sufficient desire to become so. Not when her rule was so petty."

"Petty?" I asked.

"Aye," said Mariota, warming to her subject a bit. "Petty and cruel. She is not a kind woman and rules her little flock as a tyrant would."

"Oh?"

"Yes. It was after you visited that last time. She had me do penance for speaking with you. She said I had been too forward." Mariota stopped speaking a moment and took a long swallow of ale. I did not take my eyes from her, watching her while she drank. "I knelt all night in the chapel saying my rosary, but I did not feel I had done aught amiss. And I thought on it more for a few days and was thinking that Balnahard was not the place for me."

"And so you were just walking away then?" I queried.

"Well, I was thinking on it, you see, and then something else happened and that decided me. And yes, I left. I was fair worried to do it, but I could not stay."

"*Mo chridhe,* you should have sent for me."

Mariota smiled a little wry smile.

"That is aye kind of you Muirteach, but I did not know how to be getting word to you." She paused for more ale, then continued. "I told them I would be leaving at the morning chapter meeting. I had already gathered my things into a bundle, and then wasn't I picking it up and walking away from them and out of there. And I am feeling better for having done it."

"They did not try and stop you?"

"No, they did not." Mariota made another face, as if she had tasted something bitter. "I am thinking that the abbess was as happy to see me leave as I was to go. I am not thinking she liked me much."

She took another swallow of ale, and poured more from the pitcher into her beaker.

"But I had to leave the poppy juice and the other tinctures there. They were a gift to the sisters, and I could not be taking them back from them."

"Do not be worrying about that, *mo chridhe*. Your father can get more poppy juice."

Mariota scarcely seemed to notice my comment or the endearment in her rush to tell me her story.

"She was saying I was headstrong and proud and impertinent, and would not let me work in the infirmary as I had wanted to. Not that anyone was sick, not when I first arrived. But I could have been helpful in making remedies. For all that I may not be a grand healer like my father, still I know a bit about herbs. But she would not be hearing of it, and she set me to scrubbing the floors and whitewashing the walls."

I could have said that Mariota was indeed headstrong to be running off to the nunnery and then out of it again within just a few weeks, or that she was indeed a fine healer. But I found that I was so happy to be sitting next to her in my uncle's hall with the ale loosening her tongue, the scent of her elderflower scent filling my nostrils and her sweet body sitting close to mine on that rickety bench that I did not comment. Instead I took another drink of my own ale and let Mariota continue her story.

"It is not that I do not like work, Muirteach, I will scrub and whitewash when it is needful, but it was the pettiness of her. And perhaps she is right, and I am proud and headstrong, for hasn't my own father said as much to me at times, but I could not be staying there. I could not. Not after what happened to Sister Morag."

"Sister Morag?"

"Aye, the one you brought back to Balnahard that day we were speaking." She picked up her beaker but set it down again when she found it was empty, and poured herself some more ale.

"Are you sure you should be drinking so much, *mo chridhe?*" I cautioned.

"Indeed, it's a great thirst I have tonight. And I might be regretting it tomorrow. But I am so glad to be away and out of there, Muirteach. You do not know what it is like!"

"Are you forgetting that I spent my boyhood in the priory? I am thinking I know a little about it after all those years. It was glad I was to be leaving that place, as well. But what of Sister Morag?"

"She was sore distraught that day when you brought her back. And I would have given her some of that poppy juice and warm broth and gotten her to sleep. But the abbess was saying that the devil was in her, and she must be exorcised."

"*Dia.*"

"She took her to the Stone of Penance and used the scourge on her, telling her to confess, and trying to drive the devil from her. It was cruel, Muirteach, just cruel. She was ill, not possessed."

"All the sisters did this?" I asked, incredulous.

"No, it was just the abbess, really. But the others could not stop the beating, not even Sister Euphemia, although I think she tried. And that is when I knew I could stay there no longer. It may be true that I am disobedient as she said, but I can not abide cruelty, and this was cruel, Muirteach."

"And what of Sister Morag? Did she confess? Did the devil leave her?"

"There was no devil, Muirteach, and you are knowing that as well as I do. But after the scourging, Sister Morag was weak and very quiet. They took her to the shelter of the miserable women, that one that is over on the side of the nunnery under the rocks, and she stayed there for some days. I do not know that she confessed what it was that troubled her so that day. I heard nothing about it. I am thinking the other sisters were afraid to speak of what had happened."

"Well, whatever, *mo chridhe*, I am glad you are out of it safely."

"Aye, it is good to be here. Your aunt and uncle have been kind. But I suppose I must go home soon, when there is a boat crossing the sound." She made to stand up, then sat down again abruptly. "Oh, Muirteach, I'm tipsy. The hall is spinning."

"You'd best lie down. Where are you sleeping?"

"That wee chamber where the children sleep. You know the one. I'm thinking that you slept there yourself as a lad."

Indeed I did know it well, as I knew the whole of my uncle's dun. And so I guided a very unsteady Mariota out of the hall, ignoring some inquiring looks from my uncle and Fergus. I could feel the softness of her body as she leaned against me, and I put one arm around her to help steady her steps. We made our way to the sleeping chamber where young Dòmhnall and his younger brothers and sisters lay snoring. I found what I guessed to be her mattress, stuffed with bracken and with a plaid neatly folded at the bottom of it.

"That's just grand, Muirteach," Mariota said. "It's kind to me you are." The weight of her body sagged against mine for a moment. "Oh, will this room not stop spinning—"

With that, Mariota collapsed on her mattress and I sat by her for a while, just looking at the fair, sweet form of her, until the sound of soft snoring told me she had fallen asleep. But still I sat a while longer in the darkness, watching over her while she slept.

CHAPTER 17

The next morning I told Gillespic of Gormal and her son, and how they had escaped us. He had heard some of the tale from Fergus the night before.

"Curse it, Muirteach, but you should not have been drinking any of that witch's brew. Are you such an *amadan* as all that?"

I remembered the strange vision I had had, and although I should have hung my head in shame at my uncle's scolding, I found I did not have the heart for it. The vision had been a wondrous thing, and throughout our time of searching for the witch and her son, the light of it had not entirely left me. And so I simply smiled at my uncle and agreed with him that indeed I was an *amadan* to have been so taken in. At which my uncle's bad humor evaporated like dew in the morning sun.

"Och, well, Muirteach, I would not have turned down some ale myself, after coming all that way. And I wouldn't be expecting that anyone would poison a guest. It goes against all laws, so it does."

"It was not exactly poison, Uncle," I retorted. "No one was harmed by it."

"Except that the witch and her changeling son have vanished," replied my uncle. "Perhaps they've gone back to the hollow hills."

"And in that case, Uncle, we will never be finding them and no need to be trying. But I am thinking they've simply gone to ground someplace on the islands and are not with the faerie."

My uncle snorted. "Well, perhaps we should be sending a letter to Himself at Finlaggan, and he can put some of his men to searching as well. Sure there's not a place in the Isles they could hide without him knowing of it."

"I'll go myself, Uncle. When there is a boat. And Mariota, I think, will be wanting to return to Islay as well."

"Now that she is not with the nuns. Aye, that will be fine, Muirteach. You can be taking her back, for I'm thinking you might be wanting to speak with her father soon. I've eyes in my head. You were gone from the hall a long while last night."

I could feel my cheeks flush at my uncle's words. "The lass was far gone with drink! Uncle, nothing happened. And when it does, I'll not be taking advantage of the woman when she is in her cups."

My uncle gave me a searching look. "Indeed, I do not think you will be," he said thoughtfully. "Well, we can ready a boat and you can leave today if the weather holds, or tomorrow if that squall sets in."

"Fine enough," I agreed, and left him to find Mariota.

I discovered her seated in the hall looking somewhat the worse for the last evening's drink. Her face was pale, but she gave me a wry smile when she saw me.

"And how are you feeling?" I asked.

"Oh, Muirteach, such a head I have—I do not know why I was drinking so much. Indeed I have never had so much to drink. I hardly know myself these days."

"Well, you have remedies for a sore head, don't you? I remember you giving me something when first we met."

"I was feeling so miserable I was not even thinking of it. But you are right. Perhaps I'll just be looking to see what your aunt has in the storeroom."

I followed her into the storeroom without being asked, thinking of the last time we had sat there before Mariota had gone to the nuns, and of the kiss we had shared. But it seemed Mariota was more intent on curing her headache, for she did not look at me as she rummaged among the pots and vials and herbs stored there, searching, I gathered, for some meadowsweet and other ingredients. When she had found a bunch of what she wanted, she gave it to me to hold and continued looking for another herb to add to her remedy.

"Well, this will have to do, I am thinking," she said at length.

"And what do you do with it?" I asked.

"You make a tea with it. With hot water. That will be in the kitchen," Mariota added, as though I did not know where to go for hot water. However, I did not tease her, as I could see when we got into the kitchen that Mariota's complexion was somewhat pale and green, and I did not think she'd take kindly to a joke.

"Here, let me be doing that," I said, setting some water to boil over the hearth in a kettle and taking a beaker from a shelf. "Now how much of the herb do I put in?" I asked when the water grew hot.

Mariota instructed me and then took the beaker herself and muttered a charm over it while it was steeping. When she judged it ready, she took a sip and made a face.

"It's bitter."

"As I should well remember. But I also remember that it did me good."

"Were you wanting some of it now?"

I shook my head. "I am feeling fine this morning. I think you have more need of it today, *mo chridhe.*"

Mariota drained the cup, and I told her about the plans I'd made with Gillespic to go to Islay. "Were you wanting to come?"

Mariota agreed. "It will be good to be home again. Were you seeing my father when you last went to Islay?"

"Yes."

"And were you telling him I had gone up to Balnahard? Och, I have just failed with the nuns as well. There is no reason to keep it from him."

I looked her full in the face, and spoke as clearly as I dared. "Mariota, it gives me joy that you were leaving that place. Even your father was thinking that you might not stay there. As for failing as a healer, you are too hard on yourself. That old woman spoke out of bitterness—you must not take her words to heart. You have a great deal of healing skill, Mariota." I laughed a little. "Isn't your own remedy helping you? That should prove it to you."

"It is true that I do feel better. A little. Well, we shall see about all of that. But whatever, it will be good to see home again."

And so we made ready to sail to Islay. The weather held, and we set off mid-morning, once more in my uncle's *nabhaig*, with a brisk wind blowing us across the sound. Fergus came along to help crew. As I watched the bulk of Jura and Islay loom closer, I considered the tangled threads that made this coil of confusion: Niall's murder; the faerie gold. The witch and her son, not stolen by the faerie but vanished to hide in the caves of Jura. The infant bones found in the cave near the Tràigh Bàn. The strange behavior of Sister Morag. The suspicious behavior of the Uist men and Liam MacLean, whose comings and goings still had me perplexed. The faerie lights and strangers seen dancing near the Tràigh Bàn.

"It's grim you look, Muirteach," said Mariota in a soft voice, coming to stand near me where I stared off into the horizon as if the approaching coast of Islay held the answer to my questions. "Sure it can not be as bad as all that."

"Well, one thing at least. It is better now that you are not with those sisters." I had not yet had a chance to tell of all the things that had happened while she had been at Balnahard, and I did so now, curious to hear her thoughts on it all.

"I had nearly forgotten about those bones," mused Mariota.

"Do you think it was a changeling? Are they faerie bones?"

"I am thinking not. I am thinking it was some girl in trouble."

"Aye, but from where?"

Mariota thought a moment. "Could it have been one of the sisters?"

"A sister with child? And no one knowing?"

Mariota shrugged and replied. "Stranger things have happened. Perhaps she concealed the pregnancy, and hid the baby when it was born."

"Or any girl on Colonsay could have done the same. It did not need to be one of the sisters."

"Perhaps not. But what of Gormal and her son? Their leaving does not mean he committed murder."

"No? Then why run away, if they had done nothing wrong?"

A boat on the horizon interrupted my train of thought. It looked to be fishing, although the day was not fine for that. A small boat, curiously reminiscent of the boat I had seen beached on the cove below Gormal's cave, although at this distance it was difficult to be sure. Then the boat started to move again. It looked to be heading away up the coastline of Jura from Islay. I pointed it out to Fergus.

"Aye, it could well be that witch and her son. Well, let us follow them then," agreed Fergus, and we turned the boat to pursue them.

There was a fine wind that day, and the distance between the boats grew less.

"There is one person only in the boat, a man," pronounced Fergus, after squinting at the boat. "He does not seem to have seen us."

I also had been straining my eyes to see. "Let us get closer."

A squall had blown up, and Fergus looked doubtful.

"Sailing could be dangerous in this weather. Perhaps we should make for Islay, although it would grieve me sorely to let that hag escape from us a second time."

I grinned at Fergus.

"Well, let's not let that happen. If it is her son, he will lead us to her. Can we get more speed out of the boat?"

"If you will stop making sweet words with Mariota and set your back to the oars."

And so we commenced to rowing, with a cold sea spray mixed with some sleet and whipped by the winds blowing on us as our boat skimmed over the waves.

"Look you," cried Fergus, "the boat is turning into the grand loch."

The big loch, Loch Tarbert, almost cuts the island of Jura in half. "It will be easy enough to find them there," I said. "There is no outlet."

Fergus was not so sanguine. "Perhaps, but I'm thinking there might be many wee coves where one could hide a boat if one knows the island. And the weather is none so good."

That was certainly true. The clouds had thickened. The waves had grown choppy and the wind blew cold. As we considered, the sleet changed to snow, an unseasonably early storm. I looked at Mariota, who sat shivering in the boat wrapped in her *brat*, snowflakes whitening the blue wool. I had nearly lost her life with my foolhardiness that last June.

"Perhaps we had best turn back and get to Islay before the storm worsens. We know where to look for them now. And if there is snow, it will be all that easier to track them in it."

Fergus assented and we turned the boat towards Islay, reaching the harbor at Caol Ila just before the storm came down in earnest and the sun set dimly through the snow. The weather made it difficult to reach Finlaggan, and the short day had grown late. So we decided to stay at the little inn there for the night.

My frustration made me restless, and although the meal—oatcakes and roast goose washed down with ale—was tasty, I had little appetite. I left Mariota and Fergus sitting by the smoky hearth of the inn and took myself outside. The snow still fell steadily, and it seemed there would be some inches by tomorrow. I stood, looking at the dark of the sky, watching the snowflakes come swirling out of the darkness into the light cast by the inn's doorway. Were I able to see through the glowering darkness of the sky and find some pattern in the endlessly falling snow, then I might be able to make some sense of all these tangled threads of mystery. I heard the inn door creak, and Mariota stepped outside.

"Are you not frozen, Muirteach?" The light spilling from the open doorway framed her face.

"I was wanting air," I replied a little shortly, but Mariota seemed to sense what I had not said.

"Come away in, Muirteach. The weather will be clearer in the morning."

"It is pleasant out here. It clears the head."

"Perhaps, but it is cold as well."

I turned to look her full in the face. She was shivering, biting her lower lip a little to stop its trembling, and when I drew her into my arms she did not pull away. We kissed, a long, slow kiss filled with my yearning for her, which grew fiercer as we clung together. The snow began to fall harder, but we paid it little heed.

"My love—" I started to say, but Mariota shook her head.

"Don't speak, Muirteach. Just hold me." I could feel her body tremble as she spoke.

And so I did as she asked.

After a time we began to feel the cold, despite holding each other so closely, and we entered the inn.

Fergus had gone to his bed, which was merely a pallet on the floor in the loft above, which we all were to share. So we climbed up to the loft, and lay down to sleep next to each other on the piled bracken that served as a mattress. There was no solitude, and the loud drone of Fergus's snores shook the rafters of the old inn. I lay stiffly next to Mariota and tried to close my eyes, acutely aware of Mariota lying next to me and every rustle of the straw as she moved, until her breathing softened and quieted and I could tell she slept. Myself, I slept but little that night, but it was not Fergus's snores that kept me awake.

The next morning the sun rose on a clear, pale blue sky. The several inches of snow left by the storm had already begun to melt off the thatch of the inn. Some seabirds flew across the inlet, screeching loudly, and it looked to be a fine day despite the unseasonably early snow. I thought of Gormal and her son, who had eluded us the day before. Surely by now they might be thinking, as I was, that it was a fine day for traveling and their small boat would leave no tracks.

Still, there was Mariota to consider. After the events of last summer, I felt responsible for getting her safely to her father at Finlaggan, although I was loath to take the time to get her there. But, to my surprise, I found she did not want to go.

"Muirteach," she asked, "are you not wanting to go back to Loch Tarbert to find that woman and her son?"

My guilt and relief must have shown in my face. It took little urging on Mariota's part to convince me to search for Gormal and her changeling. Fergus was awake by now and after a hurried breakfast of oat porridge we left the inn and the harbor of Caol Ila, then traveled up the Sound of Islay and set out again along the coast of Jura to Loch Tarbert.

We were glad of the faint warmth of the sun, for the morning had a chill in it. We passed the three Paps of Jura, looming high above us inland on the island. All seemed peaceful enough as we sailed along the coast, with little signs of life except the odd coney and deer that bounded away from us on the shore as our little boat sailed past. It was soon enough that we rounded the rocks at Rub´ á Bhaillein and sailed into the loch, passing a fair number of oddly raised beaches on the right of us.

Fergus had hunted with my uncle on Jura often enough and knew the island well.

"I'm thinking there is a village along the south side. We can stop and ask there if anyone has seen the two we seek."

As we continued into the loch, some plumes of white smoke rising into the air betrayed the presence of the village. We turned the boat towards the shore and pulled it up on the beach.

The village—a few blackhouses only—showed little signs of life. The inhabitants seemed to be sleeping late on this cold morning. A dog finally barked as we approached the hamlet. The door flap of the closest cottage moved and an old woman emerged, blinking her pale and rheumy eyes against the brightness of the day.

I greeted her. She appeared puzzled by our invasion.

"And what would you folk be doing here, after such a snowfall as we were having the last night? For I am thinking it is not such a fine day to be travelling."

I explained that we had been headed towards Finlaggan but had seen the boat the afternoon before. "We were wondering, just, if you had seen it. A small boat with a carved stern, with two people in it. A man, sturdily built, and a woman, older."

"And what would you be wanting with them?"

I thought, frantic. Gormal undoubtedly had friends on the island. "We were needing a remedy," I floundered.

"Needing it as bad as that?" asked the woman, unconvinced.

Mariota interrupted. "It is just that my cousin's *bairn* is sick with the falling sickness, and we are hearing of a woman on Jura who has a remedy."

"And where are you from?"

"I am of Islay near Balinaby, but my cousin lives on Colonsay. As do these people."

The old woman looked as if she wondered what a woman from Islay was doing with two men from Colonsay, and on such a snowy day, but evidently she decided this would make a tidy tale to gossip over later with her neighbors.

"Well, I was seeing a boat pass by yesterday just as the snow was falling. It might be the one you are speaking of. But there looked to be only one person in it. A man, I am thinking. It headed down that way," she said, gesturing eastwards towards where the loch narrowed a bit.

We thanked her and set off again. A brisk wind helped our boat skim along the waves, and I began to feel hopeful we would find our quarry. We sailed across the broadest section of the water without seeing any signs of the blue boat, and I began to despair of my overconfidence of the day before. Up ahead the loch seemed to end in a mass of rocky beach.

"Have we lost them? Surely they would not have sailed out, in that storm last night?"

"There is one more place we can be searching," said Fergus. "I have hunted along here, and there is a wee cove at the east end. If I was going to ground anywhere, it would be over there."

Fergus steered the boat closer along the shoreline and then through a break in the rocky shore, along a narrow channel lined with black rocks. Unexpectedly, the waters widened out again into a small sheltered cove rimmed with white beaches. And there, bright blue against the snow-covered shore, was the small boat pulled up onto the beach. However, there were no signs of life, just some tracks in the snow leading from the boat, where Lulach had walked up into the hills.

"Why would they leave their boat?"

"Perhaps there is a cave or bothy up in the hills where they took shelter. I am not thinking they would abandon the boat so easily, not when we had ceased following them. It makes no sense. And they would likely know this island well and know of whatever shelter there is to be found."

"Why not just go back to their own home on the west of the island?"

"That is a long way from here. They are doubtless thinking we are watching their home. As we should be," muttered Fergus darkly.

"Well, I am not thinking they will be so quick to abandon their boat. I am thinking we should just settle here and wait for them to return."

Mariota spoke up, "Surely they will see us when they return. And what's to prevent them then from waiting until we are leaving? Two can play at that game easily enough."

"Aye. And there is a village about a mile away, near to the coast," added Fergus. "Perhaps they sought shelter there."

"Well, let us follow them there," I said with more confidence than I felt. Already the footprints we had seen disappeared in the rapidly melting snow.

We followed the track a short distance, really, across the hills to the little village that sat near the eastern side of the island. A few houses surrounded the church, which was dedicated to the Virgin. Behind the churchyard, set a little apart, I saw an old standing stone.

The village was quiet. Smoke curled from the smoke holes in the thatch of the cottages, but most people were inside. An old man sat outside his cottage, which faced the coast, mending a fishing net, but we saw no one else. He looked up at us curiously as we approached.

"*Dia dhuit.* And it is a grand day for visitors here today, indeed it is. But a cold day, I am thinking, to be wandering about."

"Indeed," I agreed. "We are Colonsay men and came here overland from the great loch."

"Overland?" The man's eyes widened. "It is a cold day to be wandering about in the hills," he repeated suspiciously. "What is it that is bringing you here, on such a day?"

"We were seeking some people," I explained.

"And who would you be seeking?"

"That healer, from the west side of the island. We were thinking we saw her boat on Loch Tarbert and followed the tracks here."

"I am not thinking she will be here," he replied. "I am thinking she would be back at her home on a day like this. Although she will be coming here sometimes. She is saying that there are plants growing here that do not grow on the west coast where she is from. But there are no plants blooming now."

We agreed with him that there were not.

"Perhaps it would be her son you were seeing. He comes here sometimes as well."

"A big man with red hair?" asked Mariota.

"Och, yes. That would be him. And why are you wanting her at all? But shame be on my head. You are cold, and the day is not growing warmer.

"Marsali," he called into the cottage, "there are visitors here. And it is cold they are, as well."

His wife bustled outside and immediately started clucking over Mariota. "Here, I will just be getting you some hot broth. It will warm you all. The poor chick looks fair frozen. What are you thinking, to be wandering about so in the cold?"

She did not wait for an answer but disappeared inside again.

"Come away in," invited the man, whose name we discovered was Ian. And so it was soon enough that we were seated cozily inside, sipping some hot pottage from wooden bowls. I felt the warmth of it slowly settle in my stomach, while the fire warmed the rest of my body.

"And what would you be searching for on such a day as this?" inquired Ian at length.

I repeated our story about the sick child.

"I have not been seeing them lately. She is living over on the far side of the island, but sometimes she comes here. There is a well," he explained. "A healing well. It is Saint Columba's well. That old one is coming here for the water sometimes, as well as for those plants."

"The *leamhnach*," added his wife. "She will be coming over her to gather that little yellow flower. But it will not be growing now."

"So you haven't been seeing her?"

"No, but with the snow we stayed snug and warm inside. They might have passed this way. What was it you were wanting them for?"

We repeated the story about needing the remedy for the falling sickness.

"I am thinking you had better be looking for her where she bides, on the far side of the island."

"We followed their boat here."

"If they are needing the remedy so badly, perhaps they should look in that old cave before they are leaving. Perhaps she is staying there until the weather clears," said Marsali.

"What cave?" I asked.

"There is an old cave near the well and the standing stone. It is said the good saint himself stayed there long ago. After he was leaving Ireland, that was. Before he went to Iona."

"We shall check there before we leave. But as you say, it

would be better to find them at their house." And after getting directions to the cave, we left.

The track led away from the village, past the church, and up to the standing stone beyond. As we walked, I had the curious sensation we were watched, although no one stirred in the village and I could see no one. No footprints showed in the melting snow or the wet grass beneath it, now yellow from the cold of the season. After a short walk we found the well easily enough, a trickle of water coming out from a few rocks. The water tasted sweet. Despite the cold, we were thirsty and stopped a few minutes to drink. Then we began to search for the cave.

Ian's directions proved easy enough to follow, and we clambered up and around the hill a bit, to where the entrance of the cave lay hidden by some rocks.

"Here it is," I called out, and placed my hand on the black rock to steady myself as I bent down to enter. I felt a shaft of pain and looked down to see an arrow in my hand.

CHAPTER 18

I must have yelled for Mariota and Fergus were quickly by my side. The point, a flint one, had grazed my left hand, and blood flowed copiously from the wound. I observed it dispassionately, surprised at first at how little I felt it. But that instant passed and then I felt a burning pain set in.

I pushed Mariota and Fergus into the cave, and quickly followed behind them. The arrow shot had not come from inside the cave, so I reasoned we would be safe in there.

"It is that changeling," cursed Fergus, looking around. "*Nathrach* that he is. They will have been watching us the whole time."

The shot had come from farther up the hill, and as we looked we saw a figure briefly silhouetted against the sky, which then dropped out of sight, disappearing behind the hill. Fergus had already left the cave and was running after him.

"You stay with Mariota and let her tend to your wound," he yelled back at me when I attempted to go with him. "He will be getting away from us, the black-hearted one that he is."

I sat against the rocks, holding my hand, which now throbbed abominably, while Mariota examined the wound. Meanwhile, I looked around the cave. Some light from the entrance made it possible to see. The cavern, of a small size, seemed to be quite empty. But the sight of a recently burned firepit and a pile of bracken in one corner made me think that someone had stayed there, and not so long ago.

"You are lucky, Muirteach," Mariota said soberly. "Another

inch, and it might have struck and broken the bone, or torn the muscle. But this is not such a sore injury."

It felt bad enough to me, but I was loath to let on.

"I wish I had my satchel," Mariota muttered. "Perhaps there is some yarrow outside that would help it to heal. I thought I saw some by the well. Hold this against it, Muirteach, to stop the bleeding. I will go and find some yarrow."

"Mariota, be careful—there is no need," I remonstrated but, headstrong woman that she was, she had already vanished outside.

I tried to reassure myself that the shooter—Lulach it must have been—was far away by now, chased by Fergus, but I followed her outside and scanned the hills as Mariota uncovered a few poor stalks of the herb from beneath the melting snow. I felt a great relief when we were back inside the cave after what seemed a very long time.

"Here," she said, holding the dried winter leaves. "I knew there would be some yarrow someplace nearby. It survived the snow. I think it will make a poultice."

I wanted to chastise her for her foolhardiness, but she was already busy and I held my tongue.

For all that Mariota claimed to have no healing skill, she washed my injury with water from Columba's well. By the time she had put the poultice on my hand and bandaged it, the wound was feeling somewhat better.

I examined the arrow. It was fletched with hawk feathers, and the point was of worked flint, like the point we had found in Niall's back and the one that Gillean had from the *sithichean*.

Fergus appeared then, panting.

"Were you catching him?"

He cursed. "The black-hearted snake was getting away from me. But I am thinking, just, if we burn his boat, he will not be traveling so very far."

And so we rushed back to the little beach at the end of the loch. But the blue boat was already gone. We could just see it disappearing into the narrow passage that led to the greater expanse of water beyond.

We quickly boarded our own boat and pushed off, manning the oars. My anger was such that I barely noticed my injured hand. The boat was ahead, and it seemed unlikely we would catch Lulach now. We put up the sail, but the wind was against us and he had too much of a head start. We watched as he escaped us, but we followed after, out of Loch Tarbert and around to the north while the short day faded from the sky and he was lost in the darkness of the sea.

"He will not get away from us again." The determination and fury in my voice surprised even me.

"Aye," said Fergus. "Let him get ahead a bit and think we have given up the chase. We can sail well enough at night. There will be a moon tonight, and it is clear weather. I know this coast and can find their cove well enough."

We ate oatmeal mixed with water while we sailed. The moon was near full, and we had not long to wait until it rose. We traveled with the black bulk of Jura to our right and eventually the moon appeared, shining over the island and the waves of the sound. It was not too hard to find the cove where Gormal and her son lived. We saw a darker bulk, Lulach's boat, against the lighter gray of the sand in the moonlight.

"He must have assumed that we returned to Islay."

"Indeed, unless he is waiting to shoot at us from above the cliffs," I whispered back to Fergus. My hand still throbbed where the arrow had hit it, and my bad leg ached with the cold and the cramped day in the boat.

We planned to beach the boat up the shore a bit, and then

wait a few hours until the moon was setting. Then, at the night's darkest, we would surprise Gormal and Lulach. Hopefully they would be asleep. And so we sailed quietly some way past the cove and then beached the boat and made our way back along the narrow beaches, waiting for the moon to set in the west and the sky to darken.

"He will have arrows. And perhaps a dagger for closer fighting. We must get close enough so that he can not shoot. For I am thinking he is better with the bow than with close fighting."

"Aye, but he is none so bad at close fighting. Look at Liam. And Niall. And the saints only know what other weapons he might have stored in that cave."

Mariota refused to wait at the boat and I looked at her face, a white blur in the moonlight. She had a dagger and she assured me she could use it. But her face appeared pinched and nervous, and I thought I heard her murmuring a prayer as we silently made our way towards the cove. The night grew cold. We reached our position and stopped, waiting. I watched the stars swirl until the moon finally set. We silently rubbed dirt on our faces to make them less visible and started the climb up the narrow path.

I could smell peat smoke from the fire as we neared the top of the path but heard no sound. Perhaps they slept and our ruse had worked. Then I myself muttered a prayer, although I am not usually a praying man.

We reached the summit of the track and stood outside the door. In the instant before Fergus pushed it open, I heard labored breathing on the other side and realized they were ready for us.

As the door opened a rock hurtled down from within. Fergus blocked it with his shield while I cut with my long dagger, trying to wound the attacker. But I slashed at the air only, and in the dark of the cave it was difficult to see. I heard a thump and then some crashes as Fergus wrestled in the dark with someone. The glow of the peats cast a dim light in the cave. I could see Fergus struggling with Lulach, but for a moment could not see his mother. Then the woman came at us swinging a torch, swearing and cursing. I dodged the torch as she swung it at my face, then slashed at her, thinking I had cut her, but perhaps I only slashed the air again.

She threw the brand at me but Mariota, behind me, caught it up and thrust it at the old woman's face, and she shied away from the flame. In that instant, I was able to grab her by the wrists. My arms are strong and, although the arrow wound pained me, I was able to hold her there while Mariota tied her wrists together with some rope we had brought with us.

Fergus had gotten the better of Lulach and as I glanced, I saw that Lulach was bound as well. I sighed, relieved things had gone our way.

"And now," I said, "we talk."

Lulach said nothing and his mother stared obstinately ahead.

"You were killing that young boy, were you not? On Colonsay? Why? And why shoot at us over on the other side of the island?"

Lulach did not reply, so I tried my question again, speaking more loudly, and slowly, as though to an idiot.

"He'll not speak with you." His mother spat out the words. "He speaks but little."

"Does he have the power of speech?" asked Mariota.

The old woman shrugged and answered a little more calmly. "When he wishes, he can speak."

I turned towards her. "Why did you run from us, that last time we were here?"

She shrugged again. "And whyever not, if this is the way you treat us?" After a pause she added, "I did not want you to learn who I was. And then, after I told you, I was afraid."

"You are from Colonsay, are you not?"

She nodded.

"And why did you come here?"

"I could not stay there, after what they did to him."

She nodded towards her son, who sat, stolid, on the floor. "They would have killed him, to drive the faerie out of him. How could I stay there? I had to care for him and keep him safe until my own son was brought back to me. And I could not care for him there. My own parents would have tried to drive the changeling away again, thinking to bring my own son home. But I knew their efforts would fail."

"And so you came here. Why not farther away?"

She shrugged yet again. "This seemed far away enough. We were safe here for many years. We would have been safe here still, were it not for you."

"Were it not for the dead child on Carnan Eoin. Were it not for him, you would have been still left in peace."

Suddenly Lulach spoke, his voice slow and deliberate. "I did not kill him."

We all turned, surprised. After speaking, Lulach still sat as though no words had left his lips.

"Well, who did?"

"It was the shining one that did it," Lulach replied in that same flat voice.

I saw Fergus cross himself, at mention of the faerie.

"He hid him in the stones."

"And where were you, to be watching all of this? And who is the shining one?" I questioned, growing frustrated and fearful of the *sithichean* all at the same time.

"I saw it," Lulach repeated. "He shot him, then hid him in the stones."

"And where were you?"

But Lulach did not speak again.

"He did go to Colonsay in his boat." Gormal finally broke the silence. "Often he would go there to the old house and the cairn. I never went back." She shuddered. "Never."

"I am thinking there was gold on that island, hidden in the Carnan Eoin. The boy was finding a wee bracelet and another man found some things."

Gormal shook her head again and looked sadly at Lulach. "This one cares nothing for such things. For all he is of the faerie. He has his treasures, but gold is not among them."

"What treasure?" asked Mariota, curious.

"I will show you. But you must untie me."

I looked at Fergus, who scowled.

"She'll be tricking us again," he muttered.

Gormal glared back at him. "I would not. But look, in the chest. There is a box."

Fergus rummaged in the chest and pulled out a box of wood, with painted designs on it.

"There, that is his treasure."

Lulach became agitated as he saw Fergus holding the box and began to kick and struggle against the ropes holding his arms.

"You'd best put it down," observed Gormal with a sigh. "He is aye particular about it. He does not like anyone else to handle it."

"What is in it?" asked Mariota again.

"Take it and open it in front of him, so he can see."

Mariota took the box from Fergus and carried it carefully over to where Lulach sat on the floor.

"Here, look. We shall not harm your treasure. We just mean to look inside. Here, I will place it here and just open the top."

Lulach sat silent, avoiding her eyes, but he stopped struggling.

"All right?" questioned Mariota again before she opened the box.

The box was brimful of limpet shells. Lulach smiled when he saw them.

"See," Gormal said, then she repeated, "*that* is his treasure. He has no gold. Poor *amadan*. He lines them up and counts them for hours. He always has done so, even as a young child. Here, he will show you."

I nodded to Fergus, who loosened Lulach's bonds. He immediately poured the shells out, and started lining them up in rows of thirteen with thirteen rows to make a square, then started again with more shells. After he had used all the shells, he destroyed the squares and then started arranging them again, in spirals this time. The light from the fire glinted on the white shells, while he sat absorbed in the task.

"He will sit and do that for hours," explained Gormal. "It's as I said. He's of the faerie."

"They did not kill Niall," Mariota said. "Why not let them go?"

"Lulach says he did not kill Niall," I corrected.

"He is a poor *amadan*," retorted Mariota. "Look at him." We watched Lulach a moment. He sat peaceably enough, arranging and rearranging his limpet shells, totally absorbed in his task. "Do you really think he was killing Niall? An idiot like that?"

Fergus snorted. "He may not have killed Niall, but he was shooting at us right enough yesterday. As Muirteach can attest."

"Are you knowing why he would shoot at us?" I asked the witch.

Gormal shrugged. "A cornered badger bites."

"Will you come with us to Colonsay and help us?"

"And why should I be doing that? I know nothing of murdered boys or of faerie gold."

"You would say anything to save your son."

"I tell you, he isn't my son, for all that I've had care of him all these years."

"Well, your son or no, I'm thinking you might still know more than you've told us. Or he might," said Fergus, nodding towards Lulach, who continued to arrange the shells in patterns.

"He knows no more than what he's told you already. You must not take him to Colonsay. He will be afeared."

"He goes there on his own already, does he not?"

"No one sees him—he is afeared of the people there, because of what was done to him. Look," she said, struggling with her ropes. "Oh, untie me, so I can show you."

I nodded to Fergus, who complied, grumbling.

Gormal rubbed her wrists, then went over to her son. "Here, sweeting, just turn around."

Lulach obediently turned, and Gormal raised the back of his shirt, revealing a mass of old white scars and welts over his back.

"The poor thing!" exclaimed Mariota, and I thought I saw tears in her blue eyes.

For myself, I felt sick. I thought of the dead boy at Riasg Buidhe, and realized with a sharp and horrid clarity that he had not died of his fever.

"Yes," said Gormal, "that is what they did to him all those years ago when they put him to the fire. He nearly died, but I did not let death take him. I've sworn he will never go back there to that again."

The sun had risen while we talked and Mariota yawned. My eyes felt gritty as well, and my hand throbbed where the arrow had struck it the day before.

"You sleep," I told her, as I re-tied our prisoners. "I will keep watch."

★ ★ ★ ★ ★

We slept in shifts and then discussed what to do. Fergus was all for taking the two of them to Colonsay, and I agreed with him. The changeling might not know of the gold, but evidently he had seen Niall's murder. And whoever the "shining one" was, I did not think it was a faerie. Perhaps Lulach could identify him, if we could get him to speak again.

And so after a time we decided to do just that, and Gormal grudgingly agreed to the plan. However the day was already almost gone, and it seemed better to stay one more night on Jura rather than attempt the crossing so late in the day. Fergus moved our boat down to the cove below, and we ate a meager dinner of oatmeal—hot at least, this time—and prepared to stay another night.

I dozed off, then awoke suddenly. All was quiet. Too quiet, I thought. The door creaked and I called out for Fergus.

By the light of the fire we could see Lulach's place was empty. As was Gormal's. I saw a shadow cross the threshold towards the outside. "They're escaping!"

I threw myself out the door and nearly grabbed him, but a blow to my head from behind left me stumbling and Lulach far down the track to the beach. Still stunned, I turned back to see Fergus with a hastily lit torch, while Mariota struggled down the path to the beach after Gormal, who had brushed past me when I fell.

"Muirteach, be fast," Mariota called back to me. "He is making for the boat."

I sped down the track followed by Fergus, but Lulach already had gained the beach. I heard the noise of the waves as he shoved the boat into the water.

"You will not find him!" Gormal shrieked as she followed, running out through the cold waves to the boat and clambering aboard. "He has escaped you again. He can come and go like the silver ones, for he is of the faerie."

And so indeed it seemed, and perhaps Gormal herself was of the faerie, for they both had moved as silently and quickly as quicksilver.

We readied our own craft and pushed it into the water after them. Fergus pulled at the oars while Mariota and I struggled to raise the sail in the darkness. "We can gain on them easily," I reassured her. "We have a big sail, and the wind is blowing our way."

And so it seemed for a time. The sail was up, and both Fergus and I worked the oars. Despite the cold of the night, I felt sweat trickle down my face, and my breath came hard as we rowed after them while the wind pushed us closer to our quarry. Their boat, a black blur on the waves, grew larger in the distance, and I fancied I could make out the two figures aboard. And then I saw a spark flicker in the darkness ahead.

A tongue of flame, small at first, caught on the lowered sail of their boat.

"You will never catch him. I will never let you have him," came another cry from the boat, carrying across the water as we drew near. Slowly the fire grew, the little yellow and orange flames licking hungrily at the sail and gathering in strength, taking hold of wood and linen and rope.

"*Dia,*" swore Fergus as he rowed even harder, "the witch is burning the boat. She must have had a flint and steel out there."

"Muirteach, we must get closer, we must save them," cried Mariota, frantic. But we were not fast enough.

The boat burst into orange flame against the dark sky. We watched in horror as the fire burned out, listening to the crack as the mast fell down and the roar of the burning wood on top of the dark waters, and our nostrils filled with the stench of the blaze.

CHAPTER 19

We found Gormal clinging to a plank as the sky began to lighten. Of Lulach there was no sign. We dragged the woman, frozen and shivering, into our boat, and abandoned our search. Mariota wrapped Gormal in her own mantle, and chafed her hands to warm them while we sailed back to the little cove.

"But why kill her own son?" Mariota asked me after she had seen to the witch. We had returned to her cave, and Mariota had poured some hot broth into the woman who now sat, still shaking violently and bundled in a blanket, by the peat fire.

"He has gone back to his people." The old witch stirred and spoke. "The fire has driven him back to them. He was never my son. My son was taken from me long ago. I cared for him, but he was never mine. But I could not let one of the good people be captured by the likes of you." Tears streamed down her cheeks as she spoke.

"Perhaps he swam to safety," said Mariota.

"He was not knowing how to swim," Gormal answered. "He is gone, back to the *sithichean.*"

Be that as it was, we were left with fewer answers than before. If Lulach had not killed Niall, then who had? And who had struck Liam down? And where was the gold? Although we questioned Gormal repeatedly and searched her home, she insisted she knew nothing of Niall or Liam. And although we found she had many strange and mysterious things in her house, we found no gold. There was the silver bowl she had used for scrying and some crystals, but nothing else of value, not even a silver penny. But she had killed her son, if he was her son and not a changeling. So we eventually decided to take her to Finlaggan, where Himself could decide what was to be done with her.

We slept uneasily for a short while, and the next morning went down to the bay and retrieved our own boat. Some blackened timbers lay silent on the beach, but we saw no sign of Lulach. Gormal, her hands tied, said nothing.

We set out for the short trip to Islay, which thankfully was accomplished without any mishap. Mariota tended to Gormal, who stared at the waves without speaking, although at times she would laugh and cry in a way which made my own blood run cold.

"Her mind has left her," whispered Mariota to me after a particularly long outburst. She looked grieved by the whole sad affair.

We veered into the sound separating Islay from Jura just as the weather turned. We moored the boat and rented two horses, riding the distance from Caol Ila to Finlaggan. Mariota rode with me, while Fergus put the witch up on his horse. As we reached the village, I stopped my horse to let Mariota down at her father's house on the shore of the loch.

"Won't he be surprised to be seeing you after I was telling him you were with the sisters," I observed. "Or perhaps he won't be too surprised after all."

Mariota gave me a funny look, then went inside.

We continued across the causeway to His Lordship's great hall with Gormal in tow, drawing curious looks from the guards and others. The weather had turned nasty again and it was sleeting, which made the stones on the causeway slippery. The wind came off the hills and blew hard on the loch. I was not thinking our reception in the great hall would be much the warmer, for we brought no solution to the mystery and no gold with us, either.

The guards recognized me and let us enter easily enough. His Lordship was conferring with some messengers from the king in Edinburgh, and we cooled our heels in the great hall. People stared curiously at Gormal, who followed us unresisting, a blank look to her eyes but with quiet tears flooding her face. She had spoken no more about her son.

It was not busy, and despite the fire burning in the large fireplace, the high-ceilinged room was cold. We were given some warm wine and some cold meat. After the past three days, the rich taste of the wine slipped easily down my throat. Then we waited for the Lord of the Isles to conclude his business.

I had almost nodded off when some men dressed in the fashion of the capital exited from the MacDonald's privy chamber, and His Lordship's steward indicated Himself would see us there. We followed the steward into the chamber.

The Lord of the Isles was wrapped in a *brat* of soft green wool and a mantle of soft ermine skins that must have kept the chill of the day far from him. A brazier burned in the small room as well, and I was grateful for its warmth.

"Muirteach," mused the MacDonald. "And what do you have to tell me about this Colonsay affair?"

"We have brought the witch with us, my lord. Her son was killed. But I am not thinking now that he killed the young boy. Or the MacRuari."

"No? Who did then? Who killed my poor grandson?"

I told him of my suspicions.

"And what of the gold?" His Lordship asked.

"We have not found any sign of it yet. I am wondering if it is still on Colonsay. We found nothing at the witch's house, not even a groat."

"And this is Gormal?" said His Lordship. I thought I saw a

shadow pass behind his eyes as he looked at her. "From Jura?"

Gormal, obstinate, stared at the floor.

"She was of Colonsay originally. She was called Gormlaith there. Her son, the changeling, was put to the fire by her parents to drive the faerie from him, and she took the boy and ran to Jura."

"Ah, from Colonsay. And that would have been how many years ago?"

"At least twenty, my lord, perhaps longer. The man was full-grown."

"How did he die?"

"His boat burned. His mother herself burned it when they tried to escape. She said he was of the shining ones, and she would not let him be captured by us."

"She sounds crazed." The Lord of the Isles studied Gormal a moment.

"Perhaps so, my lord."

"It is a pity. I once knew a Gormlaith. It is a bonny name—blue lady."

"Yes, sire."

"I am sorry to hear of this," repeated His Lordship after a short pause. It may have been my imagination but I thought I heard genuine regret in his voice. "A mother killing her own son." He turned to Gormal. "Who was his father? There is the honor price to be paid."

Gormal still did not speak, but she raised her head and stared at His Lordship strangely.

"Her own people on Colonsay died in the plague," I volunteered.

"So perhaps there is no honor price," mused the MacDonald. "Or if there is, it should come to me here. I am the Shepherd of the Isles."

"The woman is clearly ill in her mind, sire. As was her son.

And she has no cattle or money to be paying an honor price."

"Well, perhaps some will be found. I am thinking this faerie gold is real, Muirteach. Enough real men have died for it. And when you are finding it, that can be the honor price, and it can be paid to me as the poor changeling's lord. That would be fitting."

I did not think it was so fitting, nor did I think I would find the gold. And the MacDonald's next words increased my unease.

"Is not my own grandson dead as well? So that is another reason the gold might come to me. Although," continued His Lordship with a penetrating glance in my direction, "we do not yet know who killed him."

I said nothing to that, but stared at Gormal instead, who still stood, her eyes on the floor. "And what of her?" I asked.

His Lordship shot her a look, and his face softened a bit. "Poor *amadain*. She should be cared for. The Beaton will know someone who can do it. Perhaps his daughter, the one who went over to Colonsay. Is she not with the sisters there?"

I wondered how he had heard of that. "Mariota has left the sisters," I said, "and just today returned to her father's house. She was with us on Jura."

"Indeed? Well, then, she is already knowing the woman. That would work well, I'm thinking." His face brightened. "And if the poor woman is taken to Colonsay, it may jog her wits. She may after all know something about the gold. Let her be well cared for. Fearchar will know how best to do it."

He turned to one of his retainers. "Send for the Beaton. And his daughter."

It was a short time before the Beaton and his daughter appeared. His Lordship gave orders for "the *amadain*" to be properly cared for on Colonsay. I was not sure what my uncle and my aunt would be thinking of all of that, as there was a good possibility that Gormal would be staying at the dun where she could be watched. And I doubted that Mariota, having finally returned home, would be eager to return so quickly back to Colonsay. But whatever they would be thinking, that made little difference once Himself had given the commands. And so it was that we all set out for Colonsay again the next morning.

Fergus and I took the small boat back, while the Lord of the Isles sent the Beaton, Mariota, and Gormal in a somewhat larger *birlinn* with some guards. It seemed he was not altogether trusting of Gormal, with good reason, I thought. I wondered why he went to such lengths to make sure she was cared for. Probably, I thought cynically, he wanted to make sure the gold was found and Gormal might be the best person to lead us to it.

We arrived at Scalasaig to find the larger ship already docked. The Beaton, Mariota, and Gormal had already gone up to my uncle's dun. We followed them there through the gray afternoon, although I think Fergus and I both cast a longing glance at Donald Dubh's alehouse as we passed by.

We reached the dun and passed through the stone and timber wall surrounding it, into the courtyard and the great hall. My aunt met us at the door and gave me a quick hug.

"Och, it is good to be seeing you again, Muirteach. But what a to-do! What that man was thinking of, to send that poor *amadain* here. What does he think, I am an infirmary? Better to send her to the sisters at Balnahard to be cared for, although I am thinking Mariota has had enough of them for a while. And there is that Liam still here, as well. He is awake. Are you knowing that? And speaking?"

She paused for a second, long enough to look at my expression. "But how could you be knowing?" she continued. "It is just this morning that he knew anyone. Elidh is giving him some broth. You'll be wishing to speak with him?"

"Yes, Auntie, but not before some of your good ale. The trip seemed long, and we are both thirsty."

My aunt flushed. "Shame to me for not thinking of it at once. Well, you can see what a bother I am in, with all of these people and problems."

We found Mariota, her father, and Gormal already at the table. I slid in next to Mariota on one of the benches.

"Did you hear the news?" I asked her as I reached for an oat-cake. "It seems Liam is awake."

"Aye, I was hearing something of it. It will be curious to see what he remembers. I am thinking your aunt had him in that little room the lads slept in. Where she will be putting her," continued Mariota, looking at her charge, "I do not know." Gormal sat next to Fearchar, eating very little. "What's to be done with her, I have no idea."

"You will think of something," I told her while we finished eating. "Come, let us go look in on Liam. Ask your father to come as well."

We left Gormal with His Lordship's men in the hall and went to find Liam.

We found Liam sitting up on his bed while a pretty maidser-vant spooned broth into his mouth. He looked pale and thin-ner, but his eyes had the light of self-awareness in them, and he recognized us at once.

"It is Muirteach, is it not? *Dia,* they tell me I have been unconscious for some days."

"Aye. It is closer to two weeks I am thinking."

"You are lucky," Fearchar said, "to have woken up. The injuries to the head can be a tricky thing."

"This man is Fearchar Beaton, His Lordship's own physi-cian," I told Liam. "He can examine you."

The Beaton asked Liam some questions: his name, those of his parents, where he lived, and questions about Mull. He watched Liam's eyes as he brought a candle closer then farther away from the man. He felt his grip, which seemed strong enough.

"You'll do well enough, I'm thinking," Fearchar finally said. "Stay resting another day or two, then slowly build your strength again. You may have weakened more than you know, lying here for so long."

We left him and walked back to the hall.

"He looks healthy enough," I commented.

"He looked pale, Muirteach, and thinner," corrected Mariota. "Now I must be seeing to Gormal. Father, what are you thinking would best help her to rest?"

"Poppy, perhaps? The tinctures are in my satchel," said the Beaton.

Mariota found Gormal still seated silently in the hall and led her away to the chamber where Euluasaid had arranged for them to sleep.

"I'm hoping His Lordship has not made a mistake." Unexpectedly I found myself confiding in Fearchar. "Gormal shook her confidence badly when we visited that first time. Mariota was saying she would never be a healer and that was one reason she went to the sisters. I'm hoping this will go well for her."

"I think it will go well enough," answered Fearchar. "Perhaps caring for the poor woman will help restore some of the confidence she has lost. She is a fine healer, my daughter." I noted some pride in the Beaton's voice as he spoke. "I can help her if need be, but I do not think my assistance will be necessary."

It had grown late and we were both tired. I slept in the hall that night, the Beaton in a guest chamber my aunt had prepared. But I stared wide eyed at the smoke-blackened rafters for a long while before I slept that night.

The next morning I resolved to visit Liam, who was awake and alert, and see if he remembered anything about his injury. I for one did not believe he had fallen from his horse.

The same pretty maidservant was feeding him some oatmeal when I entered.

"I was not meaning to interrupt your breakfast,"

"Now that I am awake, I have such an appetite on me. I could eat another bowl of this." He gave a winning smile to the maid.

"I will just be getting it for you," Elidh said, blushing scarlet to the roots of her reddish hair, and left us alone.

"And how are you feeling?" I asked him.

"Well enough, but I still have a pain in my head."

"That was an awful hurt. You are lucky."

Liam agreed that he was.

"I was wondering, just, if you remembered what had happened to you, how you came to be injured," I asked him. "It was a sore bad hurt to get from falling off your horse."

Liam smiled again. "What a fool, eh? You would think I had never been on a horse before."

"What could have spooked him? There was nothing amiss when we looked."

Liam closed his eyes a moment. "I am not remembering much of the accident," he said, finally opening his eyes. "I was riding fast up there by the Carnan Eoin. I had spotted a rabbit and thought to bring it back to your aunt. But it was getting darker. Perhaps the horse lost its footing? I just can not remember. The last thing I remember clearly is riding up by that cairn.

"But tell me, Muirteach, what has been happening all this time while I have been lying here like an old man. What is the news? Yon lass was saying something about Jura and a woman who killed her own son."

I told him of Gormal and the death of Lulach.

"Eh, that is a sad thing indeed. And the woman was originally of Colonsay, you say?"

I nodded. "His Lordship is thinking the woman was touched in the head, and so is wanting her to be cared for someplace. For now, Mariota is to see to her, but perhaps later the sisters will take her in. The honor price will be paid to the Mac-Donald."

"Why? Lulach, was that his name? He was not His Lordship's man."

"Indeed, but with his own mother the cause of his death, she can not be paying herself."

"And what is the honor price to be?"

I shook my head. "He had not set it when we left. Gormal did not have much, and there are no kin. She did have a silver basin. He will be taking that, I suppose." I paused, wondering whether to go on. "Although there was some talk of gold."

"Gold? *Dia!*"

"I wondered about young Niall when I was hearing of it. We searched their house, but there was nothing there, just that old silver basin."

"But you were finding nothing else?"

I shrugged. "As I said, we were not finding anything. It must have just been idle talk."

I did not tell him of the gold Euluasaid had shown me, nor of the faerie bracelet Gillean had thrown back into the loch.

Just then the maidservant returned with more oatmeal, and I wished Liam a fast recovery and left to find Mariota.

She and Gormal were sitting in the hall along with my aunt. The women were spinning. Gormal sat silently with her spindle idle while Mariota and my aunt chatted in that way women have. My uncle's dogs dozed by the hearth and altogether it was a peaceful scene.

"Och, Muirteach, we were just speaking of you," said my

aunt in a tone which made me a little suspicious.

"Indeed? And what were you saying?"

"Well, we were thinking that it is crowded here, what with that MacLean taking up the spare chamber and all, and we were not sure where Mariota and Gormal would be staying. And then I was thinking of your wee cottage down in Scalasaig. It is empty enough."

"Empty enough, Auntie, but a mess."

"It could be fixed up quickly enough, if some work was to be done on it," said my aunt pointedly. "What is wrong with it that a good cleaning and some fresh thatch would not fix?"

I looked at Gormal. She appeared placid enough now, but to my sorrow I knew she was not always so.

"I am not thinking it is altogether a good idea, Aunt," I said, not sure how much to say with Gormal sitting right there, although she gave no signs of hearing. "Two women alone—"

"Well, that is the second of my thoughts. You could stay there with them for a time. You could do for them and make sure they are safe. It is your house, Muirteach."

"Wouldn't the people in the village talk?"

"And when do they not?" returned my aunt. "I'll ask Fergus and send himself and a couple of other men down to help you. You could be starting today. The weather is fair enough for thatching, for all that it may not be the best time of the year to be doing it. And we've some rushes stored you can be using."

"But Auntie, the house is small for three," I protested. But I already knew my protests would do little good. Once my aunt got set on something, there is little that could stop her. And, to be totally honest, the thought of spending some time with Mariota, even with Gormal present, was not unwelcome.

"I'm sure you will manage. There's little enough room here with that MacLean still ill. And you would not be wanting them to stay there by themselves, for all that Aorig is next door. Plus it will let you be visiting with those brothers and sister of yours at Aorig's. That would be good for them and for you as well. And you would not want Mariota to have to take the poor woman to the sisters at Balnahard. She was just saying she did not think that would suit at all, were you not, Mariota?"

Mariota had been uncharacteristically silent during this exchange, but finally she spoke.

"I do not think the sisters can care for her adequately. Not after what I saw there." She gave me a look, and I guessed she was thinking of Sister Morag.

"And you by yourself can? I am knowing nothing of cures. And what will your father be saying about it all?"

"Aorig would be next door. She might help me watch her. It would do, for a time."

"And what of the future? His Lordship was crazy to be thinking of it," I fumed. "You can not be caring for her forever."

"Mayhap in time she will grow well enough to return home. She could harm no one there."

"Perhaps." I was unconvinced and angry that the Lord of the Isles had placed this burden on her.

"So, is that settled?" interjected my aunt, putting down her spindle and rising. "I will just go and get Fergus and see who else will be able to help. The weather is fine enough for thatching, and it would be a sad thing to waste the day."

"And inside?" questioned Mariota. She had been inside my house.

"Aye, I'll send a girl to be helping with that as well."

CHAPTER 20

So that day and the next were spent in thatching and cleaning, and by the end of it my small house was looking much better. Gormal said little but helped Mariota and Elidh, that same pretty girl who had been looking after Liam, with the cleaning and giving the inside walls a coat of whitewash, while Fergus and I thatched the roof. Seamus helped. When it was all done, I would not have recognized it for the same dwelling it was when we started. Aorig looked on with approval and fed us some tasty stews and some of her good cheese and ale when we took breaks. Finally, as the sun set red over the west on the second day, we were finished.

"Well, that's none so bad," said Aorig, looking around in amazement. "I would not have believed it would be possible."

Inside, my stool sat tidily by the hearth. Euluasaid had found a small table up at the dun, and it stood by the whitewashed wall with some wooden bowls on it. There was a kettle on the hearth where a fire had been laid, and some peats stacked up in a corner. There was a wide bracken bed for the women to sleep in, and a narrow one on the other side of the room for me. Somerled walked in, circled the fire pit, and curled up by it, very much at home.

"Well, I'm thinking we'll be comfortable enough in here," said Mariota. "But it's tired enough I am now."

"Here," Aorig put in. "Come next door. There is a stew all ready, and you won't have to be bothering about supper."

So we spent the evening at Aorig's. Gormal sat, still without speaking, and ate silently, but the rest of us had a merry time. My half brothers and half sister were doing well, and the baby, Columbanus, in particular, had grown since the summer. He was walking now and into everything. Little Sean too seemed several inches taller. Aorig and her husband sang, and even I tried my hand at a tune.

"You've none so bad a voice," observed Mariota after I had finished.

It grew late and I saw Mariota stifling a yawn. I felt awkward about sharing the cottage with Mariota and Gormal, for all that we had slept close together before. But this seemed different somehow, more intimate.

Aorig also started to yawn, and her husband said something pointedly about needing to get an early start the next day. And so we took our leave and went next door to my house.

The fire was smoldering and Mariota banked it for the night, repeating the charm: "A shining angel in charge of the embers, until the white dawn shall come again." It gave me a safe and sweet feeling to hear her; I can just barely remember my mother saying something of the sort in our little house in Islay so long ago. And then she and Gormal lay down on the wide bed closer to the hearth, and I curled up with Somerled at my feet, closer to the door, and tried to sleep.

The next morning we were just finishing our porridge when we heard a noise at the door and Somerled, who had been hoping for the leftovers, began to bark. I moved aside the door flap and saw Liam MacLean standing there.

"And so you're feeling better," I observed.

"Indeed I am, and steady on my feet as well. And himself was saying, up at the dun, your father that is," he added to Mariota, "that I might just as well go out walking. And so I was wanting to see what you had done to this place. I would not have recognized it."

It was starting to rain, and there was nothing for it but to invite him in. He was a taller man than I, and the top of his head nearly brushed the rafters so that he had to bend down a little. He seated himself on the stool by the fire, accepted the hot broth Mariota offered him, and looked curiously at Gormal.

"And so this is the witch," he observed, as if she was not seated in the room with us. Gormal glowered at him, then slowly nodded.

"You are of Colonsay?"

When she spoke, her voice sounded rusty. "I grew up here, long ago. But I have not been back. Nor did I want to be back now. Himself was ordering it."

Liam shrugged. "Himself is not here. How would he be knowing if you went back to Jura?"

"I'm thinking he would be finding out quickly enough," Mariota interposed. "But you are looking fine, Liam. Still it is a cold and rainy day to be out walking, with as sick as you've been. I'm surprised my father allowed it."

Liam shrugged again. "He said I could be up and about. Perhaps he was not actually seeing me come all the way down here." He stretched. "I am a bit tired, to be speaking the truth of it."

"Well you can rest here for a while, then go back to the dun," I said.

"Aye. But I am not all that weary. And it gets old up there, for all that that wee maid is pleasant company. I was thinking perhaps I would ride my horse a bit, up towards Carnan Eoin. I am wanting to see the place where I had my accident." He smiled. "An outing, just, it is. But it is an excuse to get out of the dun and I am wanting some fresh air."

"It is a cold day for a pleasure trip. And wet."

"Yes, but it looks to be clearing. Are any of you wanting to come along?"

Gormal spoke. "Aye. I will go with you. I used to live up there as a child."

Mariota looked worried. "Well, I will just be going with you then. Perhaps it will do us all good to get outside and away from here. Come, finish your broth and get your *brat.* You are riding, you said?" she asked Liam.

"Aye, but we can get another horse from the dun. In fact, I was not wanting to go alone, and brought another horse with me." He smiled, looking into Mariota's blue eyes, and I felt my own jaw tense. "I was hoping to convince someone here to go with me."

"Well," I said with little grace, "you now are having three people to go with you. For if they are going, I shall go along as well."

And so we finished our breakfast of broth and porridge and prepared to go. Once we got outside we could see that Liam was right; it was clearing, and some puffy clouds were blowing over across the Sound to Islay. I left Somerled at Aorig's with my half brother, who looked delighted to take charge of the dog for the day. The sun was warming the land, and we rode up the track past the standing stones and Bríde's well until we reached Loch Fada, then traveled west and up towards Carnan Eoin. Gormal was seated behind Liam on his horse, while Mariota sat behind me. I relished the feel of her body pressed against mine, for all that I thought this was a fool's outing. As we rode, we talked.

"I am hoping that the poor woman will tell us more if she is someplace familiar. Perhaps it will help her to deal with her sad memories."

"Umm," I muttered, unconvinced. "I am not knowing why Liam MacLean should interest himself in Carnan Eoin."

"Well, he was saying he wanted to see where he fell from his horse."

"I am not thinking he fell."

We climbed up the track leading between the two hills until we reached Beinn Beag. There we dismounted from the horses and tethered them. Gormal walked up to the ruined hut, followed more slowly by Mariota, Liam, and me.

"This is it. This is where I lived with my parents so long ago." Tears streamed down her cheeks.

"And your son, he lived there with you?" I asked.

"Aye. He was born and was a bonny babe. But then after a time, the faeries took him. One night it was that I dreamed of the shining ones. They were standing over the cradle and singing a strange song. I saw them there, but I could not move to save my son. And the next morning the babe was not well. He stopped looking at me and did not speak. He had trouble at the breast. He did not nurse well. I prayed and prayed that the *sithichean* would give my own son back to me, but they never did."

"And so you cared for the changeling."

"Aye, I did." She was crying in earnest now. "We stayed here with my parents until the lad grew older. And he grew stronger as well. We tried all kinds of remedies and herbs, but he remained a changeling, seldom speaking. The other boys mocked him and he would fly into violent rages, but he never hurt me. My parents were afeared of him, for they were old, and he was big. And then one time, I had left him with my mother while I went to get some herbs. My parents put him to the fire to drive out the faerie. They laid him in the fire pit."

"The poor thing," whispered Mariota.

"I heard his screams as I was coming home and gathered up the boy. He was alive and still breathing, but sore wounded. My parents told me it was the only way, but I knew that was not true. That night, late, I wrapped the boy up and carried him away and out of there and stole down to the beach and took a boat."

"And you went to Jura," I finished.

"Aye. He was a changeling, but I had to care for him. Else they would never be giving me my own son back. But the good folk, the *sithichean,* never found us. I was thinking that they would know, being of the faerie, and would be pleased how I had saved their babe. But they never came and gave me back my own son."

"And your own parents?"

"I was never seeing them again, nor this place, until today. I heard later that they had died when the Black Death came." Her voice broke.

She sank down on the turf inside the ruins of the cottage and began to wail, rocking back and forth as she keened.

Liam, who had been listening to her story with interest, sat down against the ruined wall of the cottage, looking pale.

"It is a sad story. And a strange one. The poor woman. Think you she is grieving for her child that was stolen, or her parents, or the changeling that died in the fire on the boat?"

"All of them, I expect," I said.

"Shush," said Mariota. "We must let her cry." She sat down next to her and tried to take her hand, but Gormal pushed her away and continued rocking back and forth, sobbing.

After a while Mariota rose and left Gormal's side. "I wish I had some poppy for her," murmured Mariota to me. "Or that my father was here."

"Indeed, I'm thinking your father will be none too pleased to see his patient has stolen away out today. Liam is not looking well either."

Gormal's keening died down to a softer crying, but she still sat crouched in the ruined cottage, shaking and rocking back and forth.

Liam spoke. "Poor *amadain*. Perhaps you could be borrowing something for her from the good sisters up the way. And I am feeling weak as well. I think I have overdone things. I will just rest here while you go, and I will sit with the poor woman for a while. It would not be taking you long to go up to Balnahard, for some remedy for her."

"And what makes you think they will be giving me poppy juice?" asked Mariota sharply. I did not think she wanted to go back to the nunnery, and I confess this gave me some joy.

"Or perhaps they could send someone back with some supplies."

"Wouldn't it be better to just return to Scalasaig? She could be cared for there more easily."

"Look you," said Liam, surprisingly forceful, "the poor woman is overwrought. And I myself am too tired to make that long journey back now. I must rest a while. I will stay with her and watch her. Muirteach, you go on with Mariota. Do not worry. I will watch her like a hawk and make sure no evil comes to her."

And so Mariota and I mounted the horses and rode up to Balnahard. The abbess was none too pleased to find us on her doorstep, but grudgingly she agreed to send Sister Morag back with us, along with medications.

But when we arrived back at Beinn Beag we saw no sign of Gormal or Liam. They both had disappeared as though stolen away by the faerie.

CHAPTER 21

The hut was deserted, although as we looked more carefully we could see some footprints in the turf that seemed to lead up to the cairn where I had found Niall's body.

There, next to the cairn, we saw Liam.

He had somehow pushed one of the large stones on the side of the cairn aside and now dug frantically in the dirt beside it. There beside him on the grass lay the gold. Glowing bracelets and torques, all twisted and shining, like molten sunbeams caught in the grass, and some smaller items like the odd piece that Euluasaid had shown me. Flat necklaces with strange faerie marks etched on them in rows spilled onto the ground, looking like the crescent moon fallen to earth.

Liam heard us and looked up from his digging. "Muirteach, it's back too soon you are. I was thinking it would be taking you longer than all that to come back from Balnahard."

The pieces came together, too late.

"So it was you that killed the young lad after all," I accused.

"I did not want to," Liam protested. "I told them stories of the faerie hills, but the foolish boys took them seriously. And then young Niall came and showed me that wee bit piece of gold he had found and he told me where it was he was finding it. And I myself had been thinking it was all just stories to entertain the *bairns* with.

"Then I had to have it all, you see. For I am to be married soon, to a sister of the MacLean of Duart. It will be a good match. And I was needing the gold for that. So I had to kill the poor boy, for he would have told of it."

"So it was you that killed Niall. What of the faerie arrow?" I asked him.

"They're easy enough to find and not hard to put on a shaft."

"And why wait so long to get the gold?"

"Well, I could not be getting it while I was sick in bed," Liam returned conversationally.

"And who was it that hit you on the head?"

"It was that changeling—her son. He used to come and count the gold. He'd pull it from the hiding place and count it and put it back again. I'd seen him in the past when I'd been visiting with Morag in the hills. Then Niall found the piece of gold and told me of it, and I followed them there that day. I watched while the other boy left him and while Niall dug at the cairn, and then I fired the arrow that killed him and hid the body. But I had to go back to Mull. It was some time before I could return here. Not until that day we went hunting and you left me here was I able to come back. I waited for a long time, and finally I saw that changeling come and push the stone aside. He took out the gold and counted it, arranging the pieces in strange patterns, and then he hid it again and pushed the stone back on it. He seemed agitated. I am thinking he recognized that one piece was missing. And he found me and felled me with a rock. At least I am guessing that's what happened. I am not remembering the fall too well."

He turned to Sister Morag, as if he had just realized she was there. "But here is Morag," he said. "Why have you brought her here?"

I turned and stared at Sister Morag, who stood pale and trembling next to Mariota.

"I thought you were dead," she accused Liam.

"Aye, and well I might have been. But I am not, as you see."

"I thought you were dead," she repeated.

Liam shrugged.

"But what of your fine promises?" Sister Morag continued. "Those that you made to me. Now that you have the gold, we can leave. We can get away from here."

"And why would I be leaving with you, when I am already betrothed to the MacLean's sister?"

"But you said—"

Liam looked sad. "Aye, Morag, I know. I loved you those long years ago in Mull and since, after your family sent you here to the sisters. But think, woman. Where could we be going, a defrocked nun and myself? There's no place we could go. With the MacLean's sister I'll have a fine life."

"I killed for you. I killed our baby—"

"But what else could you have done?" returned Liam with an unnatural logic. "You could not be keeping a *bairn* with the sisters."

Sister Morag leapt towards Liam like a wild thing or *bean-shìdh* herself, her *sgian dubh* drawn, but he was too quick for her. His own knife slashed towards her throat as I tried to stop him, but Liam was surprisingly strong for one sick so long. We fell to the ground and grappled together in the turf, rolling over and over as I pushed against his arms, trying to keep his dagger from my own throat.

He tried to force his knife closer to my flesh. "There, Muirteach. I am not wanting to kill you, now. Let me go and take the gold with me, and there'll be no harm done to anyone."

"Except for Niall and now the sister," I retorted, thrusting the dagger back towards his own face. "No. You will come with me."

He struggled against me and I continued holding him down, although I began to tire and my grip on him grew weaker.

Liam sensed his advantage. He shoved hard against me, pinning me to the ground, and of a sudden I felt his iron at my throat again.

"But look you, Muirteach, if you will not be reasonable, well, then I shall have to kill you. For this gold I will have. I have already committed mortal sin for it. What's one more?"

I pushed back, attempting to break away. But he had the upper hand, and I feared for my life.

A shadow passed over us and a huge rock came crashing down on Liam's temple. He crumpled in a heap atop of me, and I felt his breath against my face. Then the breath stopped and I rolled out from under the weight of him to find Mariota standing, white-faced, looking down at his body.

"Muirteach—" she said, her breath coming ragged and fast. "I have just killed a man."

CHAPTER 22

I stood unsteadily and then held her tight, rejoicing that I was still alive to see her and smell that elderflower scent she had, and feel the pounding of her heartbeat against my own chest. "You have saved my life." We clung together a moment more, her body trembling. Perhaps my own body shook as well while we held each other there.

"No now," I said again, "you saved me." Then I thought of our other concerns.

"What of the sister, of Morag?"

Mariota stepped back from me, took a deep breath and seemed to steady herself. "She will survive. I stopped the bleeding. It was a glancing blow."

I looked and saw Sister Morag sitting amid the gold, one hand pressing a cloth tightly to her neck. She seemed far gone into shock, her face pale, not registering the fact that her man was dead. For dead Liam most certainly was.

"Muirteach, where is Gormal?" asked Mariota slowly, turning to look down the track that led to the Tràigh Bàn. "I did not see her anywhere."

"I do not know. Perhaps she has gone to ground someplace. She grew up on this island."

"But, Muirteach, we must find her."

We searched and called and saw no sign of her, although we scoured the Carnan Eoin and the Beinn Beag. The sun began to head towards the west, and I thought of the treasure still lying there.

"Come. We must do something with this gold before word gets out and the entire island is here to help themselves."

We had packed the gold in a pouch, wrapped in soft woolen cloth, and left Liam's body on the ground there by the cairn, decently covered by his *brat*. Carrying the pouch, we escorted Sister Morag back to the convent. She did not speak. We left her in the care of Sister Euphemia, telling her briefly what had happened, and we made our way back to Carnan Eoin.

Liam's body still lay as we had left it. I had wished it would disappear, spirited away by the *sithichean*, but it remained there stubbornly.

I turned away from the cloth-covered mound that had been Liam MacLean, and walked with Mariota some ways away from the cairn.

"What a strange day," Mariota mused. "I can not be the same person I was when it started."

I guessed she thought of Liam.

"No, but you saved my life."

There was a fallen stone close by, its surface weathered gray and yellow with lichen. I sat down on it, and drew Mariota down next to me. She still shook, with cold, or shock. I put my arms around her and held her against my own warmth.

"And it was all for the gold. And greed," continued Mariota after a moment. "But it is beautiful, is it not?"

"Indeed," I said, letting go of Mariota and pulling the pouch out. "Let us look at it, before it goes off to His Lordship."

We spread the treasure out between us on the stone and marveled again at it all. Shapes so fine and thin they must indeed have been made by faerie goldsmiths, with strange designs on them—triangles and diamonds—engraved into the rich shining surface of the gold. The golden, glittering heart of it, so rich and warm it was, it made my own heart leap within my chest just to look at it.

"Here, *mo chridhe,* put some of it on. I would like just to see you in it, just for a moment."

Mariota demurred but I insisted, and soon she was arrayed in it: a golden crescent at her throat, bracelets on her arms, and over it all her flowing hair shimmering like the gold itself.

The sun, well past the midday point in the sky, glinted on her ornaments as its beams found their way through the clouds, and sent a glowing brightness all around her. She looked like some goddess of old.

"Eh, Muirteach, it is lovely. I feel like a queen. Such a lovely thing to have such evil intertwined with it. The deaths of so many—"

"I know, dear heart."

"Well," she said with a sigh, "I will have to take it off now. Come, Muirteach, we can not stay here all the night. They will come looking for us."

"I know," I repeated, my mind on something else entirely.

Slowly Mariota began to take off the bangles and wrap them in the cloth. "And so it is to go to His Lordship?" asked Mariota. "That is a pity. It has brought nothing but suffering with it."

I nodded, thinking of Niall. And of Lulach and his mother. "That is what His Lordship was ordering. And I am thinking he will see that he gets it."

"But it is the faeries' gold!" The words burst out of Mariota vehemently and I turned, surprised by the passion with which she spoke. "It will only bring ill to others, Muirteach."

"And how will we be explaining that to the MacDonald? For I am thinking he is a greedy man himself, for all that he is a lord. No, now, we must give it to him. And how would we be explaining Liam's body to him and to the MacLean?"

Mariota's face fell. "It was a fancy. That was all. Come, let us go back to the dun."

We placed Liam's body on his horse; the horse did not want to carry its burden—I could tell from its widened nostrils, but being well trained it eventually did. We carried the gold and Mariota sat in front of me on my horse, which did not complain. Neither did I, enjoying the warmth of her pressing against me. We led Liam's horse behind us.

The sun was low in the sky, flaming all the western sky a brilliant red. We slowly picked our way down the rocky track that led downward from Carnan Eoin. I felt Mariota move suddenly.

"Look, Muirteach," she cried, "over there—"

I turned my head to follow her gaze, and there, down on the sands, I saw a moving figure.

"Who's there?" I called. The figure seemed to melt away in the growing darkness by the shore.

"Muirteach, I think it is Gormal."

"Aye, and if so, well, we must go and get her."

We rode down onto the beach, and our horses made their way through the sand towards where we had seen the figure. We soon caught up with her. Indeed it was Gormal. She stopped when she saw us approach and waited until we reached her, her back towards the pounding waves on the beach.

"What happened to you?" Mariota asked. But Gormal had a wild look in her eyes and did not reply. "We were afeard," continued Mariota, "that Liam had tried to harm you. He is dead. He tried to kill Muirteach."

Gormal stood there, still unspeaking. "Come now," said Mariota soothingly. "We will go back to the dun, and then back to Scalasaig. Come," she said, dismounting, as did I. Both horses stood quietly, waiting. "Come away with us."

Finally Gormal spoke. "What have you done with their gold?"

"It is safe, here, with us."

"It does not belong to you. It is theirs; their son was guarding it for them. You must not be stealing their gold. That's what I tried to tell that other one. He would not listen to me. Then I ran away, for the vengeance of the shining ones is a terrible thing. I did not want to be there to incur their wrath."

"Their gold is safe enough," I said. "Here, we will show you." I dismounted, and opened the pouch to show her. "Here, come and look for yourself."

Gormal approached closer and examined the pouch. She bent her head over it.

"Let me see more of it. It has caused so much sorrow."

And fool that I was, I took the pouch and held it towards her.

She looked closer. "Aye, it is here." She paused and her eyes got a faraway look in them again. "I remember when he came, years ago, to this same island," she said, after an instant.

"And who was that?" I asked, reaching out to take the pouch back from her.

Gormal laughed, ignoring my gesture. "Himself it was, His Lordship. And a fine young man he was then. He had come visiting, been out riding and lost his way a bit. And there I was in the hills with the sheep. The mist came down all around us, like an enchantment, and we sought shelter in an old dun. He took me then, and didn't I have a fine son by him. But the faeries took my son away. And His Lordship shall not take their gold, or they will never be giving my son back to me."

Then, like the shape-shifters of the *sithichean,* she clutched the pouch to her and ran with it towards the waters of the bay. Mariota and I both tried to catch her, but she was fast and had the strength of the mad. She wriggled from our grasp like the water horse and ran into the waves, floundering as the water reached her chest and neck, but she continued deeper into the sea.

"Muirteach, we must stop her. She means to drown herself."

Gormal was far out in the water now, not heeding our calls. "And take the gold with her, too," I said as I stripped down to my tunic and entered the water.

CHAPTER 23

I am a strong swimmer. The water was icy so late in the year; the waves pounded against me, and I could not find her in the black coldness of the bay. The tide was going out and pulled me with it to where I judged we had last seen her, but I could find no trace. Gormal had vanished beneath the waves, and the gold with her.

I dove and dove again, seeking her in the water. But the tide was strong and must have pulled her out to sea. When I glanced towards the shore, I found I also was being pulled far from land. I could barely see the shore, a different blackness from that of the water.

My arms and legs grew numb with the cold, and I heard Mariota calling faintly. Finally, frustrated and helpless, I gave up the search and turned and started for the land. It was slow going, the tide pulling against me. I stroked harder as the fear grew in me that my own feet might not touch the land again, and that the sea would claim me for her own. Then suddenly, I felt the welcome sand beneath my feet and I emerged, shivering with cold and fear, to find Mariota had started a bonfire on the beach.

Mariota rushed towards me and wrapped her arms around me, walking with me towards the fire.

"My love, I thought you were lost too. You were out there so long, and I could not see you in the blackness." There were tears running down her face, and I kissed them from her cheeks.

The light had attracted some islanders from near Àine's cottage. They stood curiously by the fire while I limped, trembling violently from the cold, over to the flames. Gratefully I warmed myself, although the core of my being felt like it would never be warm again. Mariota wrapped my *brat* warmly around my shoulders as I stood there shaking in the darkness. One of the islanders offered me a drink from a leather flask of *uisgebeatha*. My hands trembled as I reached for it. I felt the welcome burning of the drink down my throat and clasped the flask a moment, feeling the texture of the surface, before I handed it back.

"We will come back and search at daylight. But I am not thinking we will find her there." The last rays of the sun flamed the western sky to red as I spoke.

"Nor am I thinking we will find the gold. She has given it back to the shining ones. Poor creature," murmured Mariota. "I failed her in the end."

"White love, you must not think that. You tried to stop her. We both did. She was crazed and had the strength of the mad."

"And I nearly lost you as well. Thanks to the Blessed Mother and all the saints you came back to me." Mariota clung to me by the fire, and I held her warmth against me. The dusk of the early evening faded to black night.

"Yes, I heard you calling. That turned me back.

"Although," I said, breaking away from her for a minute with a wry smile, "I'm not thinking the MacDonald will be too happy to hear the gold is at the bottom of the sea. I may be sorry indeed that I did not drown when he hears of it."

"She was mad," Mariota said. "And I killed a man today." She shuddered. I could feel it as I held her while the flames burned lower on the beach. "Muirteach, let us go home and be away from this place."

And so we left and rode back to Dun Evin by torchlight.

We reached Dun Evin late and had to call out for the gate to be opened for us. People wondered at the body of Liam, and my aunt clucked and made noises over both Mariota and myself. She fed us hot broth as though we were both invalids, wrapped us in warm plaids and set us by the great hearth in the hall, all the while marveling at the events of that day.

"To think I harbored that viper at my own breast," she muttered. "And trusted him. No, no, I never trusted him. There was always that look in his blue eyes. And all the while he was here eating my food and drinking my drink, full of his sin and his guilt. With never a whisper of it. To think he himself killed poor Niall . . ." She wiped away her tears with the back of her hand and went off into the kitchen, leaving us to speak more privately with my uncle and the Beaton.

We recounted the events of the day and both men listened intently.

"Himself will not be pleased at this," said my uncle, drinking some more *uisgebeatha.*

"Yes, well, he should be pleased that the murderer is found."

"I am thinking of the gold. He will hold us accountable. Or perhaps he will try to drain the bay to find it again."

"Even His Lordship can not drain the seas," returned the Beaton. "He will not be pleased, but what is done is done. And he is a canny leader. If you can convince him that you have told the truth, I am thinking he will accept your words. He has no choice and in fact has other concerns on his mind, what with the MacRuaris to contend with the now. They are stirring up trouble again. Were you hearing that his son, Niall's father, killed that Raghnall? He accused him again of murdering the lad, and they came to blows. And now both clans are at each other's throats."

I felt a pang of guilt. "If I had suspected Liam earlier, perhaps it would not have come to that. I failed to find the murderer until too late."

My uncle looked at me strangely. "But you did find him, Muirteach, and he a child-killer. He'll be burning in hell the now, and justice that is."

"Aye," added my aunt, who had returned from the kitchens. "And glad I am of it," she said with unusual vindictiveness. "My poor wee *bairn*." She left again, her eyes brimming with tears.

"Well, perhaps this news will put a stop to that feud," the Beaton commented. "If His Lordship can speak reason to his son."

"Let us hope he sees reason about the gold as well. And is believing Muirteach's tale," replied my uncle.

I had not thought that he might not believe our story. "Well, he can search all he wants, but he'll not find the gold," I said with more bravado than I felt. "It's at the bottom of the bay now or swept out in the sea, and Gormal's body with it."

"Aye, and half the island will be watching the beach for any gold that might wash up. Or corpses," said my uncle darkly.

It was late, and I suddenly realized how exhausted I was. "Uncle, if you can spare a torch, I will just go on back to the village," I said, stifling a huge yawn.

"You're not wanting to sleep here?" asked my uncle. "It'd be no trouble."

The events of the day had unnerved me and I wanted quiet. And Somerled was still at home.

"No, I think I'll be going down there. I must see to my dog. But thank you." I stood to go, surprised when Mariota stood as well.

"I'm going with him, Father," she said to the Beaton, not once looking at me. Her father gave me a look, and I could have sworn there was a smile hiding there. He sighed.

"Aye, Mariota, I thought you might be." He embraced her. "Go, my treasure, and with my blessings."

Saying little, we left the dun and rode the short distance down to the village. I keenly felt Mariota's presence as she sat before me on the horse while we made our way down the steep hill leading from the dun and down the road to Scalasaig. Most of the houses were already darkened, and it was quiet. We entered the cottage and I struggled to start the peats burning, my fingers suddenly all thumbs. Finally a little bluish-yellow flame started up along one edge of the peats and gradually grew in strength. I stood up and faced Mariota across the fire.

"It is a poor enough place I have brought you to, my love," I said.

"There is no other place I would rather be than here with you."

Then I crossed the cottage to where she stood and I took her into my arms.

EPILOGUE

His Lordship did near drain the bay in his efforts to find the gold. But Gormal's body washed up on the shore some days after she walked into the bay, which lent some credence to my story, as did the witness of the islanders who had seen me emerge from the sea. Sister Morag also had the wound on her neck to prove our story. I did not mention the tiny bones in the cave, nor did anyone else.

If any of the islanders found any faerie gold on the beach of the Tràigh Bàn, they were too canny to speak of it. In the meantime, the MacDonald near tore the cairn apart stone by stone in his effort to find any remaining gold, but none was ever found. Liam's family on Mull paid an honor price for Niall's death and that mollified His Lordship somewhat, although that gold went to Niall's father, and he was himself owing the MacRuaris for Raghnall's murder.

Mariota and I were handfasted soon after, before Christmas. We stayed in Scalasaig until after the Christmas feast, and then returned to my farm in Islay in the new year. But later that spring my uncle called me back on business to Colonsay. As I disembarked, I saw two sisters wearing pilgrims' hats and cloaks as people waited to board ship in Scalasaig. One was Sister Morag.

I greeted her. I had not seen her since that bloody afternoon in November. She looked much different: thinner, and somewhat calmer.

"You are going on a pilgrimage?" I asked her.

"Yes, to Santiago de Compostela in faraway Spain. It is said that a pilgrimage to that shrine will help atone for one's sins, and I have many sins to atone for."

I thought of those small bones I had found in the cave. And of Gormal and her strange son, and of poor Niall and Liam. "We all have sins," I said. "But I wish you a safe journey and a safe return."

She smiled faintly. "As to it's being safe, we shall see. But I must thank you, Muirteach. For you saved my life on that sad day."

She smiled again, and boarded the ship with her companion, and Colonsay saw her no more.

ABOUT THE AUTHOR

Susan McDuffie's childhood interest in Scotland was fueled by stories of the traditional clan lands of Colonsay and the McDuffie clan's traditional role as "Keeper of the Records" for the Lord of the Isles. On her first visit to Scotland she hitchhiked her way through the Outer Hebrides, at length arriving on Colonsay, and the initial seeds for the Muirteach mysteries were planted.

Susan has visited Colonsay several times and extensively researched the Muirteach MacPhee mysteries. She lives in New Mexico, sharing her life with a Native American sculptor and four rambunctious cats. Susan loves to hear from readers and can be contacted via email at s.mcduffie@att.net or through her website www.SusanMcDuffie.net. She is currently working on Muirteach's next adventure.